HER RELUCTANT AMISH HEART

PAMELA DESMOND WRIGHT

Recycling programs for this product may not exist in your area.

ISBN-13: 978-1-335-52911-4

Her Reluctant Amish Heart

For questions and comments about the quality of this book, please contact us at CustomerService@Harlequin.com.

Love Inspired
22 Adelaide St. West, 41st Floor
Toronto, Ontario M5H 4E3, Canada
www.LoveInspired.com

HarperCollins Publishers
Macken House, 39/40 Mayor Street Upper,
Dublin 1, D01 C9W8, Ireland
www.HarperCollins.com

Printed in Lithuania

1 2 3 4 5 6 7 8 9 10 LIT 28 27 26 25

"I didn't mean to make you feel bad," Anika said.

Swallowing, Elam forced a shrug. "It's not you. It's me. I've been so mad about the judge taking my driver's license that I couldn't think about anything else. But the truth is, I did it to myself. I knew that street wasn't the place to race, but I let my pride get in the way."

A beat of silence passed before Anika spoke, her voice barely above a whisper. "I caused a lot of problems, too...because I was mad."

Elam turned his head, uncertain if he'd heard her right. Her words were so quiet, they nearly slipped past him. "What do you mean?"

Peeking over her shoulder to make sure they were alone, Anika leaned in closer. "I knew I wasn't supposed to do something, but I did it anyway."

His brows rose. "Oh?"

She hesitated, her fingers knotting into the folds of her apron. "I've been so scared." Voice faltering, she trembled, as if struggling to get the words out. "I think *Gott* is punishing me..."

Pamela Desmond Wright grew up in a small, dusty Texas town. Like the Amish, Pamela is a fan of the simple life. Her childhood includes memories of the olden days: old-fashioned oil lamps, cooking over an authentic wood-burning stove and making popcorn over a crackling fire at her grandparents' cabin. The authentic log cabin Pamela grew up playing in was donated to the Muleshoe Heritage Center in Muleshoe, Texas, where it is on public display.

Books by Pamela Desmond Wright

Love Inspired

The Cowboy's Amish Haven
Finding Her Amish Home
The Amish Bachelor's Bride
Bonding over the Amish Baby
Her Surprise Amish Match
Her Amish Refuge
An Amish Widow's Hope
Her Reluctant Amish Heart

Visit the Author Profile page at LoveInspired.com.

But they that wait upon the Lord shall renew their
strength; they shall mount up with wings as eagles;
they shall run, and not be weary;
and they shall walk, and not faint.
—*Isaiah* 40:31

This book is dedicated to my beta readers, Andrea (@judy.ann.loves.books) and Carrie Schmidt (@meezcarrie). Your feedback during the earliest drafts made all the difference. I'm deeply grateful for your time, support and encouragement.

To my editor, Melissa Endlich, and my agent, Tamela H. Murray—thank you for walking beside me on this writing journey. Melissa, your guidance and dedication sharpen my words and bring out the best in every story. Tamela, your wise counsel gives me the strength and confidence to continue pursuing the calling to write these books. I am grateful for the ways you both guide, uplift and inspire!

Chapter One

"Hey, Elam, want to race?"

Glancing over at the El Camino idling in the next lane, Elam shook his head. "Not the time or the place, man," he called back.

"What's the matter, Mueller?" Chris Weaver goaded. "You chicken?"

Elam smirked back, the taunt igniting a familiar spark. "Hardly."

Chris leaned across the passenger seat, the cocky grin on his face illuminated by the dim glow of his dashboard. "You're just afraid you'll lose driving that junk heap." He revved his engine, the roar breaking the night's quiet.

Elam eyed the sleek vehicle. Chris bragged endlessly about its big-block V8, claiming it was unbeatable. Stylish and fast, sure enough. But his truck had a Hemi engine, solid and reliable, with enough power to give it a run for its money.

"Mine can run circles around yours," he threw back.

Chris snorted. "Prove it." He jabbed a finger toward the end of the lane. "Just a sprint down. The loser buys the other a six-pack."

The gauntlet was thrown.

Elam felt the pull of competition. Growing up in Wisconsin Amish country, he'd learned to suppress his impulses. But since leaving the church, he'd found himself chasing every activity the *Ordnung* condemned. Now twenty-two, he was restless, hungry for something more than the daily grind of work. But like many small towns, Humble didn't offer much in the way of excitement. The only real entertainment came from what young folks made for themselves, and racing had become the unofficial pastime. Late at night, the empty streets stretched ahead, an open invitation to put the pedal to the metal. Plus, the chance to put Chris in his place only added to the enticement.

"All right," he agreed. "You're on."

Chris threw a thumbs-up. "Let's do this."

Lifting his foot off the brake, Elam eased his pickup forward. *Just a quick run.*

After a long shift at work, he'd earned a little fun. His last ticket should've been a warning, but the dare was too tempting. His old truck wasn't much, but in his mind, he was behind the wheel of his classic Dodge Challenger. Recently done with its restoration, he hadn't raced the car. But he planned to. Soon.

A minute stretched out, tense and slow.

Then the stoplight flipped to green.

Both engines roared to life.

Elam felt the asphalt grip beneath his tires as his truck lurched forward. "Come on, baby. Show him you've got what it takes!"

The two vehicles zoomed ahead, neck and neck. Then, in a sudden burst of speed, the El Camino launched forward, pulling ahead by a full length.

Determined to go faster, Elam slammed the accelerator to the floor. The truck's motor whined in protest but kept on going.

Closer…closer…

A flash of movement up ahead at the intersection caught his eye. A boy on a bicycle zipped through a stop sign, oblivious to the danger hurtling toward him.

Elam's blood pressure dropped. Time seemed to freeze.

"Whoa!" he yelled, foot slamming on the brake pedal. The truck jolted, tires screeching in protest as the metal frame groaned beneath the pressure. With every ounce of effort, he fought to keep control as the truck shuddered to a halt.

But Chris wasn't as lucky. Tires squealing, the El Camino skidded wildly, fishtailing across the pavement.

In a desperate attempt to avoid the collision, the rider threw himself to one side, tumbling onto the asphalt seconds before the car struck his bicycle. A sickening thud rang out as twisted metal slammed into the vehicle's windshield. The sound was horrifying, echoing through the still of the night.

Frozen in shock, Elam gripped the steering wheel. His pulse thundered in his ears. For a moment, he couldn't move. Couldn't breathe.

"Oh, God…please let him be okay…"

Shifting into Park, he slammed open the truck door, sprinting toward the scene. Chris was already out of his car, his face pale, eyes wide with panic. The boy lay crumpled on the street, a pained whimper escaping him.

Trembling, Chris paced, clutching his head. "I didn't see him!" he cried, voice sharp with panic. "He just came out of nowhere."

Fighting a wave of nausea, Elam didn't answer. Dread settled over him as he took in the damage. Dressed in Amish clothing, the boy's face was pinched in agony. Breath coming in sharp bursts, his right leg bent at an unnatural angle.

"Call 911!" he barked. "He's hurt, bad!"

"I'm on it." Chris fumbled with his cell phone, hands shaking as he punched in the number.

Mind spinning, Elam dropped to his knees. "Hey, you're going to be okay," he gritted, not sure if he was speaking to the victim or trying to convince himself. As he surveyed the scene, the realization hit him like a punch.

This wasn't just an accident. It was a disaster.

And the worst part?

The trouble was just beginning.

* * *

Elam sat rigid at the defendant's table, his hands clenched into fists beneath the worn surface. Not so very long ago, he'd been footloose and fancy-free, living life on his terms. One stupid decision had changed all that. Now, he had to pay the piper.

Behind him, wooden benches groaned as the handful of spectators settled in. He risked a glance over his shoulder, a flicker of foolish hope dying in his chest. Not a single member of his family had come. He hadn't expected them to. Choosing to leave the church, he'd walked away from their world. The rift between them was deep, something he doubted could ever be repaired.

Only one familiar face stood out in the sparse crowd. Of course, Bishop James Graber would be present. The church elder always showed up when someone from the Plain community found themselves on the wrong side of the law.

Unable to meet the older man's gaze, Elam focused on the judge. A middle-aged man with a hard-set mouth and wire-rimmed glasses, Judge Lawrence Hartwell thumbed through the case file, his expression unreadable.

"The court has reviewed the details of this case," Hartwell began, his voice echoing through the space. "Reckless driving that caused bodily injury. And as a result, a fourteen-year-old was seriously injured."

Elam's pulse hammered. He still couldn't block out the memories haunting him since that night. After Chris had called 911, an ambulance arrived. Paramedics stabilized the boy as onlookers gathered. Police came, too, their flashing lights casting an eerie glow over the scene. By the time it was all over, both he and Chris were slapped in handcuffs and taken to jail.

The judge's gaze settled on him. "Do you understand the gravity of what you've done, Mr. Mueller?"

"Yes," he muttered.

His attorney elbowed him. "Speak up, son."

Elam cleared his throat. "Yes. I do."

Judge Hartwell leaned forward, clasping his hands together. "It's only by a very narrow margin that your foolish actions didn't end in a manslaughter conviction. As it stands, it's only being charged as a misdemeanor. Still, based on your past driving record, it's clear that your decisions were not only irresponsible but dangerous, too." Frowning, he added, "Do you have anything to say for yourself?"

"I'm sorry," he answered honestly. "Chris and I were just having fun. We didn't mean for anyone to get hurt."

"That's a start, but remorse isn't enough," Judge Hartwell said, turning to the prosecution. "Does the state wish to make any remarks before sentencing?"

The district attorney, a tall woman with a sharp gaze, rose from her chair. "Thank you, Your Honor." She turned toward Elam, her expression unforgiving. "It's clear from the defendant's history of tickets that he has a problem with speeding. We cannot tolerate behavior that puts others in harm's way." She paused for a moment, her eyes steady on Elam as if daring him to disagree.

"Go on," the judge said.

"The state recommends a firm sentence not only to hold Mr. Mueller accountable but also to send a message that this sort of behavior will not be tolerated." The DA's statement rang through the courtroom.

Elam bristled with discomfort. He'd never intended to cause any harm. But there was no going back now.

His attorney rose to his feet, his voice calm but determined. "Mr. Mueller is committed to making amends, not just to Nathan and his family, but also to the broader community," he argued. "Given that this is his first serious offense, we respectfully ask the court for leniency."

Judge Hartwell nodded. "I've heard from both sides," he said. "I'll render my decision shortly."

And there it was. The moment he'd dreaded. He'd told himself a dozen times the accident wasn't his fault, that Nathan Glick shouldn't have been out so late at night. And the teenager had ignored the stop sign, which made it partially his own doing. But the court didn't see it that way.

I should have just said no to Chris and gone home.

Too little, too late.

The courtroom fell silent as Judge Hartwell adjusted his glasses and went over the paperwork. After a brief pause, he spoke again. "Sentencing will commence as follows. First, your driver's license is hereby suspended for one year. You are prohibited from operating any motor vehicle during that time. Do I make myself clear?"

Elam clenched his jaw, swallowing a groan. This was worse than he'd expected. Losing his license would cripple his ability to work. Still, it wasn't up to him. He didn't have a say.

"Understood."

"Second," the judge continued, "you are sentenced to one hundred hours of community service. Given that you were raised Amish, the district attorney has recommended that this service be carried out under the supervision of Bishop Graber. She has spoken with the bishop, and he has voluntarily agreed to oversee your progress."

James Graber rose from his seat. "I will, Your Honor," he said, his voice steady. Clad in a plain black suit that spoke to both humility and strength, he carried himself with quiet authority.

Elam winced. *Oh, great.* Just what he needed, being under the bishop's watchful eye. A constant reminder of the faith he'd tried to outrun but could never fully leave behind.

Judge Hartwell kept going. "Third, you will pay a fine of five hundred dollars." Penalties meted out, he added, "Any failure to meet the community's standards or to complete your hours will result in jail time. Do you understand?"

He nodded. "Yes, Your Honor."

"This is an opportunity for you to learn to make better choices, Mr. Mueller," the judge concluded. "I suggest you don't squander it."

"I'll do my best. Thank you."

Silence prevailed, ending the session.

"We are adjourned." With that, Judge Hartwell's gavel came down with a sharp crack.

Snapping his briefcase shut, his attorney rose. "You got off easy, kid," he said under his breath. "If Bishop Graber hadn't come forward on your behalf, you'd be cooling your heels in jail right now."

Elam again cast a wary eye behind him. The way the Anabaptist community handled matters through elders and a strict set of guidelines was something the *Englisch* world didn't always grasp. Over time, the courts had learned that as long as the congregation held its members accountable, they would step back and let the church leaders take the reins. Yet if a situation ever escalated beyond the bounds of their faith, the law wouldn't hesitate to intervene.

His chest tightened. Though he'd left the church, he wasn't excommunicated or shunned, for he'd never taken the baptismal vows. Still, years had passed since he'd stood before the congregation's most respected authority. Now every stern look from the bishop felt like a measure of judgment, weighing his every move.

He'd escaped the rules…but not the reckoning.

"This thing just isn't working."

Expression tight, Reuben Glick's voice cracked as he fumbled to maneuver his wheelchair into position at the head of the table. The wheels snagged on the edge of the rug, halting his progress.

"Slow down and have patience," Anika said, guiding her father past the obstacle.

"I feel useless." His hands gripped the armrests as if willing himself to move past his limitations. "It's hard, being stuck in this thing all day."

Anika bent, locking the wheels in place. "I know it's hard. But you're still here. *Gott* must have a purpose for you, even if we don't see it yet."

Daed shook his head. "Purpose? What kind of purpose can a man have when he can't take care of his *familie*?"

Aching inside, Anika stepped back. Once a towering figure, *Daed* had always been the cornerstone of their *familie*, his broad shoulders capable of carrying any weight life placed upon them. But everything had changed in a single, shattering moment. Her mother and older brother were gone. And her father, who had always seemed invincible, was a broken man.

"You're still strong," she said, trying to reach him. "Stronger than anyone I've ever known."

He gave a faint shake of his head. "If only that were true. But it's not myself I worry for." His voice cracked slightly. "It's you. You've taken on so much. I see it, even when you think I don't."

"I'm fine," she countered, her denial more reflex than truth. "I just want you to concentrate on getting better."

"I'm trying, *mei maedel*," he sighed. "And I'll keep trying."

Forcing a smile, she nodded. "I know you will." But inside, it tore at her, watching her father fight so hard and getting nowhere. Standing by, helpless, was the hardest part of all.

Since the accident that had paralyzed him, *Daed* had done his best to live a normal life. Despite his physical limitations, he still insisted on getting up and getting dressed, as he always had. With a few modifications, he was able to wear the same shirt and trousers he usually favored. His favorite work boots covered his feet. After the accident, neighbors came together to make the *haus* more accessible. They widened doorways, built ramps, and added sturdy handrails in the washroom. The updates helped, but adjusting to his new reality was a slow, uphill journey.

"I want to walk again," he continued, voice tight with emotion. "I'm praying that *Gott* will send me a healing."

Anika gave his shoulder an encouraging squeeze. "Me, too."

Before *Daed* could reply, a sudden clatter echoed down the hall.

"Help!" a familiar voice bellowed. "I need help!"

Anika released a weary breath. "I'll be back."

Turning, she hurried down the hall, her skirts brushing against her legs. The faint creak of the floorboards echoed under her shoes, a reminder of the countless tasks that still awaited her attention.

Twisting the doorknob, she stepped into her brother's bedroom. Early-morning light filtered through the curtains, softening the starkness of the plain room. Nathan was still sprawled in bed. Stretching from thigh to ankle, the cast on his leg inhibited his mobility.

"*Guten morgen*," she greeted, helping untangle him from his blankets. "How did you sleep?"

Face scrunching, he groaned. "Terrible. This thing is awful." Swerving his bicycle to avoid a speeding driver, he'd broken his leg.

Anika winced at the stark white cast. A few days earlier, she'd heard both the drivers involved were finally due to face sentencing. Thankfully, Nathan wouldn't be called to testify; the DA had assured them the crash evidence was more than enough to secure convictions.

"Let me help you." Her brother's injuries had turned her already overwhelming days into an impossible balancing act, stretching her time and energy thinner than ever.

"*Danke*." Hands gripping her shoulders, Nathan swung his legs over the side of the bed. The size and awkwardness of the cast on his leg made him clumsy, and he wobbled as he tried to steady himself.

"I don't like this," he said through a grimace. "I feel like a baby."

Anika's brows furrowed. Her patience, already worn thin, snapped. "Doesn't matter what you like. This is what happens when you make foolish choices."

Nathan scowled, hurt flashing in his eyes. "Just stop it."

"Stop what?"

He let out a heavy breath. "You know what. You're still mad because I snuck out of the house that night."

She bristled. "Why shouldn't I be? It was late. Too late for you to be out, and you knew it."

Nathan hung his head. "I shouldn't have done it," he admitted. "I just needed to get out for a while. To feel like a normal kid, you know?" His voice broke, the words tumbling out faster now. "I wanted to buy a soda, maybe a candy bar, ride my bike…" Faltering, tears welled up in his eyes. "I miss *Mamm* and Jason so much. And *Daed*… He isn't *Daed* anymore."

His confession hit like a blow, pain and fear woven into his every word. For all his attempts at being mature, he was still very much a *youngie*.

Anika's anger ebbed, leaving behind the familiar ache of guilt that had shadowed her since the accident. Barely eighteen, she felt decades older, worn thin by worry and the endless cycle of chores and obligations. The washing, the cooking, the care of her *daed* and *bruder*—all of it fell to her now. Each morning she rose before dawn, and each night she went to bed bone-tired, knowing that tomorrow would demand just as much.

The weight of her responsibilities pressed hard, but she had no other choice but to bear the weight. There was no one else to lean on.

"Everything's different now," she said. "You've changed. I've changed. And *Daed* most of all." The truth hung between them, undeniable and raw. They were all broken now, forever marked by what had been lost.

Helplessness clouded his eyes. "We'll never be who we used to be, will we?"

Her shoulders sagged. "*Nein.*"

Silence settled over them, broken only by the quiet sniffle as Nathan wiped his face. "What do we do? How do we get it back?"

The ache inside intensified. "I don't know."

Nathan stared ahead. "I've been praying, but it doesn't seem like anything is getting better."

Anika pursed her lips. The accident in the barn had changed everything in an instant. *Mamm* and Jason were gone, lost in the blink of an eye. *Daed* had survived the terrible collapse—but he was paralyzed from the waist down. Doctors said there might be a chance he could walk again, but they didn't know for sure. Countless prayers had been offered up by the community, asking *Gott* to restore her father's strength and heal his broken body. Thus far, heaven had remained silent.

"It's easy to get discouraged when it seems like nothing's happening," she said, giving the only answer that made sense. "All we can do is keep trying. *Daed* needs us both to take care of the farm."

Nathan sniffled again. "Now I'm no help at all."

Anika's stomach clenched. "Things will get better," she said. "Do you need help getting dressed?" She reached for the crutches leaning against the wall.

Pride flaring, her brother stiffened. "I can manage."

She turned slightly, as if distancing herself from the sting. "If that's what you think." Handing him the crutches, she added, "I need to get breakfast on the table."

"I'll be there as soon as I can," Nathan said, reaching for his clothes.

Anika didn't reply. Closing the bedroom door, she headed

toward the kitchen. A tight knot formed in her chest as she walked. Instead of easing, everything felt like it was unraveling.

A flood of self-pity washed over her. *How do I get through this?*

She felt herself slipping, the edges of her control fraying. If something didn't give soon, she was certain she'd shatter into a million little pieces. She was desperate for a lifeline, something to grab on to, to pull her back from the edge.

But all around her, there was only emptiness.

"Everything okay?" *Daed* asked.

His question yanked her back. "Fine," she said, moving toward the stove. "Nathan just got tangled up." Though they had a few modern conveniences, electricity had never made its way to the old *haus*. Nestled in the countryside, they relied on simpler means: propane for the appliances, oil lamps for light, and wood fires for warmth.

"I regret so much has fallen on your shoulders," *Daed* said, apologizing again. "I know you haven't had a minute to yourself in a long time."

"I like staying busy," she reassured him, checking the oven. To her relief, nothing had burned. "It makes the day feel like it goes by faster." As was her habit, she'd gotten up early to prepare the first meal of the day. The kitchen was filled with warmth and inviting scents. A batch of sourdough biscuits had been her first task. Now done, they were perfectly golden. Atop the stove, the rhythmic sputter of the metal percolator promised a warm, comforting drink.

Plating the biscuits, she set them on the table. A pan of creamy sausage gravy followed, completing the simple but hearty meal.

"Sorry it took so long." Opening a cabinet, she reached for the earthenware mugs, filling each with the rich, steaming *kaffee*. The warmth of the liquid seeped through the ceramic as she carried the mugs to the table, placing one in front of her father.

"Everything looks *gut*, *lieb*," he said, taking a sip. "Sometimes I think you cook better than your *mamm*." As he spoke, a rare smile of remembrance broke through his weariness.

Anika's heart warmed. "I try."

A loud clatter echoed down the hall as Nathan struggled to maneuver out of his bedroom, the thud of his crutches punctuating each step. His cast bumped the edge of a tall cabinet, sending a basket of rag scraps tumbling to the floor in a cascade of fabric.

"Have a care, please," she called. "I've already got more than enough to do without cleaning up more of your messes."

Nathan hobbled in, his movements awkward as he lowered himself into a chair. "It's hard to get around on these things."

Anika sighed. "I know it's not easy. But try to be careful, *ja*?" Wiping her hands on her apron, she pulled out the chair across from him and sat down.

Her brother nodded, looking sheepish. "I'll do better."

Satisfied, Anika gestured toward the spread on the table. "I hope you're both hungry. I made plenty."

"I'm starving," Nathan said, eyes lighting up as he reached for the biscuits.

"*Nee*," *Daed* admonished, his tone firm and disapproving. "Not until we've said our prayers."

Nathan pulled his hand back, cheeks flushing. "*Ach*, sorry."

Daed's stern expression softened. "Since you're so eager to eat, maybe you should lead us in the morning prayer."

Nathan gulped, eyes wide in surprise. "Me?"

He nodded. "Go on."

With a nervous grin, Nathan cleared his throat and then bowed his head. "Lord, bless this food and our home today..."

He didn't get the chance to finish. A sharp knock on the front door drew everyone's attention.

"Wonder who that is," *Daed* muttered, attempting to maneuver his wheelchair away from the table. "Far as I know, we're not expecting any visitors today."

Anika stood, her hand pressing briefly against her father's shoulder. "I'll get it." Hurrying through the living room, her chest tightened at the thought of a stranger arriving, disrupting the fragile routine she'd built. They weren't expecting company.

She yanked open the door and froze.

There, on her porch, stood Elam Mueller.

Anika's breath hitched. He had no business coming around, not after what he'd done. One of the drivers responsible for her brother's shattered leg and ruined bike, he should've had the sense to stay away. Yet here he was, standing like he belonged. Seeing him made her pulse jump for all the wrong reasons.

"What are you doing here?"

Elam shoved his hands deep into his pockets, his expression caught somewhere between hesitation and resolve. "Thought I'd stop by…see how Nathan is."

Anika recoiled. Heat surged through her, like wildfire catching dry grass. Over a month had passed since the accident, and now he just showed up, as if time had somehow wiped the slate clean.

"You've got no business being here," she snapped, her voice edged with steel. "And you're certainly not welcome."

"But—"

Unwilling to hear another word, Anika's hand shot out. She slammed the door with a force that shook the frame.

"Go away," she spat under her breath. "And stay away!"

Chapter Two

James Graber sat behind a heavy oak desk, his hands folded atop an open ledger. His office was small but orderly, the scent of aged books and lamp oil lingering in the air. A soft breeze drifted through the open window behind him, stirring the curtains and carrying away some of the lingering mustiness.

Elam sat stiffly, trying not to let his nervousness show. Being called before the bishop was always an anxious time for folks, and he was no exception. He wasn't part of the church anymore, but he still understood the weight an elder's words carried. Respect was nonnegotiable. Whatever resentment he carried had to stay buried.

Just get through it, he told himself. *Then move on.*

"I know it's a burden to answer to me," Graber opened in a firm tone. "However, Judge Hartwell has placed you under my supervision. I expect you to fulfill every minute of your sentence. No excuses."

Elam's fingers curled into his palms. "Yes, sir."

"I trust you've taken some time to reflect on the damages you inflicted."

"I have."

"*Gut.*" Graber said, looking over his ledger. "After some consideration, I've decided to place you in the Helping Hands program."

"Helping Hands?"

"It's a new partnership between several churches, Amish and *Englisch.* As you know, *Gott* commands us to care for the most vulnerable, and this program provides support for the elderly and disabled."

"That makes sense."

"To fulfill your hours, I've set a schedule," the bishop said. "Five hours a day, six days a week. I understand you're between jobs, so best to get it done."

Elam's ears warmed. "Ah…yeah. That…that works," he mumbled. "What will I be doing?"

"To start, I've enrolled you in the Meals on Wheels program, which Pastor Mark Jensen oversees."

"Okay."

"Since Pastor Jensen will only need you for a few hours in the afternoons, I'm also assigning you home-care duties."

He tensed. "Like what?"

"You'll be helping a disabled individual with daily chores, lending a helpful hand wherever it's needed."

Relief swept over him. That didn't sound so bad. "All right. I can do that." The sooner he burned through his court-ordered hours, the better. Every minute he spent doing volunteer work brought him one step closer to freedom.

"I'm glad you think so." Graber flipped through the ledger, then paused, peering over the top of his glasses. "You'll be assisting the Glick family."

Elam's stomach clenched. "That might not be such a good idea."

"Explain."

"I stopped by their place after I got out of court," he explained. "Thought I'd check in on Nathan…" Embarrassed, he trailed off, reluctant to say more.

"And?"

"Anika slammed the door in my face," he grumbled. "Didn't even let me finish a sentence."

Bishop Graber's brows rose. "Did she now?"

"Yeah. Told me to go away."

"Did she?" the bishop repeated, voice mild but probing.

Elam's irritation flickered. "Yes, she did."

The bishop studied him a long moment, then asked quietly, "Tell me something—why did you wait so long to check on Nathan?"

The question stopped him cold.

"I—I don't know," Elam stammered. He probably should have reached out to the Glick family sooner, but uncertainty and guilt had kept him away. The pending hearing had given him an excuse, a reason to stay away. However, excuses didn't erase what he'd done; they only made the distance feel longer, the silence sharper, the regret more suffocating.

Bishop Graber leaned back in his chair. "Looking at it from Anika's side, she probably wasn't feeling too welcoming. You can't blame her for that."

Elam's jaw tightened, irritation prickling under his skin. The bishop was right, but that didn't make it easier to hear. "Fair enough," he said. "I know I messed up. But I'm trying to make things right. The least Anika could do is give me a chance."

The bishop gave him a sharp look. "Do you even understand what that family has been through?"

"Nathan broke his leg," he said, shrugging. "That's bad, sure, but it's not the end of the world."

"That's the least of their worries."

"Oh, yeah?"

Graber exhaled. "You don't know, do you?"

A prickle crawled up Elam's spine. He'd gone to the Glick farm with the best of intentions. But Anika's wary gaze and the ice in her voice had made it clear that she wanted nothing to do with him.

"Know what?"

The bishop's mouth pressed into a firm line. When he finally spoke, his voice was quiet but heavy. "There was an accident. The barn loft collapsed, and a stack of bales came down." He hesitated. "Ada and Jason didn't make it."

Elam's breath caught. "I didn't know."

"About six months ago. Reuben was caught under it, too. His spine was crushed. He's been crippled ever since."

The tightness in Elam's chest expanded. A strange stillness settled over him. No wonder Anika wanted nothing to do with him.

"I never heard about it." He hadn't meant to drift away from the people he'd grown up with. But somewhere, between the long hours spent towing and repairing cars and the nights hanging out drinking with his friends, he had.

"The *familie* has been struggling," the bishop continued. "Especially Anika. She keeps herself holed up, tends to her father and Nathan, but at great cost to herself."

"I'm sorry," he said.

"Reuben's in a wheelchair, and Nathan's laid up," Graber explained. "Except for her *grossdaadi*, Anika doesn't have anyone to help with chores. She could use a hand until Nathan recovers."

Elam straightened a little. "Anything they need, I'll do it." Pausing, he added, "You think Anika will accept my help?"

"There's only one way to find out." Bishop Graber's stern expression softened, the weight in his eyes lifting just a little. "I'll arrange for us to visit tomorrow. I'll speak with Reuben myself and plead your case."

"Yeah. That sounds like a plan." Whatever it took to unsnarl the mess he'd made, he'd do it.

Reviewing his notes, the bishop adjusted his glasses. "Now that we've settled that, there's another matter I'd like your thoughts on."

"What's that?"

The older man tapped a pencil against the stack. "Seeing

that you're a mechanic, I'd like to get your thoughts on a few things I've been considering."

"Fire away."

"We need to be more organized in our efforts to expand our charity work. That's why we're considering moving into a dedicated meetinghouse to coordinate our efforts."

"That makes sense."

"We need a place for volunteers to gather, where supplies can be stored and distributed. We've also discussed the possibility of getting a van for transportation, especially for our elderly and disabled members. Believe it or not, I'm aware that a buggy isn't always practical when someone has a doctor's appointment out of town or some such."

"Wait, you're serious? A meetinghouse and van? For the church?"

"Why not? We've always found ways to adapt while staying true to our principles. This would be no different."

Elam straightened. "I never thought I'd hear you say something like that."

"The Lord tells us there is strength in flexibility," Graber said, chuckling. "I may be old, but I'm willing to bend when it comes to trying new things."

"I think it's a good idea." Traditionally, most Plain communities didn't have a singular space for church services or large gatherings. Instead, the town was divided into districts, with families taking turns hosting services. It was a system that had worked for generations, fostering a sense of shared responsibility. However, the logistics of maintaining this practice no longer made sense, especially during harsh weather or busy seasons. A central meetinghouse wasn't just practical. It was a way to ensure everyone could gather without undue hardship.

"It's still a while from happening," the bishop cautioned. "We have a location in mind, but it needs remodeling. Also, we'll need to find the right vehicle, something in our budget."

Elam leaned forward. "I can help. If I check used car lots, I'm sure I can find something dependable." He hesitated briefly, then added, "I could handle the maintenance, too. If any repairs are needed or stuff like that. Call it my way of giving back."

Eyes crinkling, a smile broke the solemnity of the older man's expression. "That would be appreciated."

"You can count on me to find something affordable."

"Excellent. The *Leit* agrees this is a good step toward better caring for our most vulnerable," the bishop said. "Tradition's hard to break, but most folks recognize when change is needed. We pay *Englischers* to rent their vehicles and drive us. Might as well invest in our own transportation. We've also agreed unbaptized members may do the driving."

Elam perked up considerably. A lot of Amish youths got their probationary licenses during *rumspringa*.

"I never imagined things would change this much."

"You'd have known all about it if you came to church," Graber said. "It's been a topic of discussion, and we've had some lively debates, to be sure. All voices were heard, and every concern was addressed to the satisfaction of all. The *Ordnung* isn't carved in stone. It can be updated or clarified as needed."

Chastened, Elam winced. "I know I've been out of touch."

"How do you intend to remedy the matter?"

He hesitated. To the Amish, the church was more than just a place of worship; it was the foundation of their lives, the heart of their community. Their faith in God wasn't just a belief. It was the very cornerstone upon which the Anabaptist movement had been built.

"I might try coming, um, sometime."

Bushy brows lifted. "You speak like it's something to fear."

"Maybe I do. It's hard when you feel like you don't belong anymore."

"Why do you think that is?"

"I don't know," he confessed. "Most of the time I'm not sure how God fits in today's world."

"I can see why you might feel that way. Things do move fast, and people are always chasing something newer, louder, bigger. But we can take comfort in knowing the Lord doesn't change. He's the constant. Always present, always relevant."

The words struck like a bell. "I guess I have forgotten that."

"I won't twist your arm," Graber said. "*Gott*'s word is free to all, to be taken up when you're ready. Do with that what you will."

Fingers curling into his palms, Elam sucked in a breath. "I'll think on it."

Even as he spoke, regret pinged hard. Eager to chase the freedom to do what he wanted, he'd allowed himself to drift away from the values he'd been raised to cherish. Home. Family. Faith. He'd let it all slip away just to satisfy the desires of self. Now, all he had left was a hollow emptiness, a gnawing ache he didn't know how to fill.

Emotion tightened his throat. Maybe serving his sentence in the Amish community wouldn't be as unbearable as he'd imagined.

Elam was back, and he'd brought the bishop with him.

Anika reached for the kettle, hands shaking as metal clinked against the faucet while she filled it with water.

Her mind raced, spinning in circles. *How could he? How dare he!* What had he told the bishop? Was she in trouble? Confusion and fear stormed through her. Had she done something wrong? Was she about to be reprimanded?

Setting the kettle on the stove, she pressed her palms into the counter. "Calm down." It didn't work. The tension in her muscles only tightened.

Wiping damp palms on her apron, she glanced toward the front room. Muffled voices reached her. Her father had welcomed both visitors, inviting them in to sit a spell. By the sound of it, the men were having a cordial conversation.

About what?

She intended to find out.

Reaching for the tea, her fingers brushed the edge of the canister before pulling back. Would the bishop even want something to drink? Should she wait for him to ask?

Nay, she decided. Serving tea would give her a reason to join the conversation, to show she was prepared to be gracious. Thankfully, Nathan wasn't home. Earlier, *Poppi* had come by to take him to his doctor's appointment. The follow-up was crucial to determine if his leg was healing properly and whether his cast needed any adjustments.

Squaring her shoulders, Anika arranged cups on a tray, her hands trembling. Letting the tea leaves steep in the boiling water granted her a few precious moments to steady her nerves. She wasn't about to let Elam Mueller see her falter. Not this time. If he thought he could waltz back, bringing his confidence and easy charm, he was sorely mistaken. This time, she would meet him with a serene smile, a calm voice, and the unwavering hospitality *Gott* expected.

Balancing the tray, she paused briefly in the doorway, composing her expression before stepping into the room.

Elam was perched on the edge of the settee, his posture relaxed. His hair was slightly tousled, and his gaze flicked up to meet hers. His eyes held a shadow.

Regret, maybe? Or was it just her imagination?

Bishop Graber sat nearby, his sturdy frame and gentle presence commanding respect. "You'd be helping the *boi* out if you gave him some work around the farm."

Seated in his wheelchair, her father rested his hands on his knees. "We could use the extra hands," *Daed* agreed. "Between Nathan being laid up and me in this chair, things aren't getting done as fast as they used to."

Grip tightening on the tray, Anika's stomach sank. *No, no, no!* With *Poppi*'s help, she'd managed fine. Elam didn't need to be here. She didn't want him hanging around.

Elam straightened, clearing his throat. "I'm willing to do what's needed. Just say the word and it's done."

Intending to argue against the idea, she set her expression like a mask: composed, polite, but brittle. "I've brought tea." Placing the tray on the table, she avoided Elam's pleading looks.

"*Danke*, daughter," *Daed* said, nodding. Accepting the cup, he cradled it between his large hands.

Anika distributed the drinks. "I think we're taking care of things fine. *Poppi* has been helping, and Nathan will be on his feet soon."

"Your grandfather has his place to take care of," *Daed* reminded. "It's not right to keep asking him to put aside his chores."

Anika froze. Her pride recoiled at accepting Elam's help.

"We've managed."

Daed set his cup down, the soft clink against the saucer breaking the charged silence. "Most everything's already fallen back on you, and I've seen how much you're struggling. I think the arrangement would be helpful to all concerned."

"I don't know..." she murmured, not ready to agree but unwilling to argue.

"I can tend to the animals and do repairs," Elam added, spreading his hands. "Whatever you think will be most useful."

Anika's chest tightened. His tone sounded sincere, and there was humility in the way he sat with his shoulders bowed.

"I believe Elam is trying to better himself," the bishop prodded. "He deserves the opportunity to prove himself."

"I hold no grudge for the accident," *Daed* said. "We're taught to forgive, as *Gott* has forgiven us. To deny Elam that mercy would be to deny our Lord's command. Forgiveness is not for us to measure. Only to give."

A lump formed in Anika's throat. She had no wiggle room to refuse. How could she tell her father *nay* when forgiveness was the cornerstone of their faith?

Still, she didn't answer.

The silence grew heavy with expectation. The decision weighed on her, and she had to say something.

"I suppose we could use him," she allowed. "Maybe an hour or two a day. But no more than that, I'm sure."

"Glad to hear it." Bishop Graber stroked his gray beard. "I'm sure the details can be worked out as needed."

Anika forced a smile. "Of course." Like it or not, she was stuck with Elam.

"While I'm here," the bishop continued, pausing to take a quick sip from his cup, "I wanted to share an update about our progress in securing transportation for our handicapped members."

Gaze brightening, *Daed* leaned forward. "I've been hoping you'd have news."

Anika perked up. The process of getting her father out of the *haus* was difficult. The narrow opening of the buggy, with its high sides and low seat, made it impossible to fit a wheelchair inside, meaning that he had to be physically lifted from the chair and placed inside. The men who helped struggled to move him without causing pain or drawing attention to how frail he had become.

Her father never complained, but she could see the humiliation in his eyes. He hated being a burden. After a few times, he'd given up going anywhere, skipping his appointments. Save when it was their turn to host services, attending church had also become a thing of the past. Ever mindful of her father's limitations, Bishop Graber often came by to share his sermons and other news throughout the community.

"Is it going to happen?" she asked.

Graber nodded. "The funds have been raised, and we're

ready to move forward." He looked at Elam. "Elam's offered to use his skills to find a suitable vehicle. As you know, he's a mechanic by trade. I've no doubt he'll find something we can work with."

Daed clapped his hand against his knee, his face lighting up. "That's the best news I've heard in a long time."

The bishop nodded. "The *Leit* has agreed to amend the *Ordnung* to allow the use of gas-powered vehicles when necessary. And I'm aware many younger folks do learn to operate a vehicle, so we might as well put the skill to use."

Anika felt a ripple of surprise, followed by a rush of gratitude. This shift felt like a small but meaningful victory. It wasn't just about the vehicle. It was about the community coming together in new ways, trusting one another in ways they hadn't before. It was truly a lifeline, one that would help her father regain a sense of normalcy.

"*Danke*, Bishop. It will be so *gut* for *Dat*."

"I'm looking forward to going again," *Daed* added.

The bishop nodded. "It won't happen overnight," he cautioned. "But I trust Elam to handle it as he sees fit."

Elam grinned. "I'll get started as soon as I can. If there's one thing I know, it's cars. I'll find just the right one. That's a promise."

"I've no doubt." Graber's eyes twinkled. "You might not think so, but I believe *Gott*'s working in the most wonderful ways."

"Amen," *Daed* murmured. "This is the best news we've had in a long while." He looked at Anika. "Why don't you show Elam around? It'll give him a chance to see where his help is needed."

The air thinned, shrinking the world around her until everything around her felt twisted and tight. Suffocating.

Anika's stomach twisted. The last thing she wanted was to be alone with Elam, especially not outside. Just stepping past the threshold of her home, into a world that felt too vast and overwhelming, made her pulse quicken. Expectation pressed down, leaving her no choice but to comply.

"*Ja.*" She gestured stiffly for him to follow. "This way."

Walking with heavy steps, Anika led him through the kitchen. Hand trembling, she reached for the screen door and pushed it open. The warm summer air hit her, and she recoiled. Sunlight dappled the ground in patches, casting bright spots through the branches.

It was too much. Too bright. Too open.

Anika froze at the top of the stoop. She hadn't entered the barn since that horrible day when she'd found three members of her family buried beneath the collapsed hay bales. Only Nathan had been spared, safe by sheer chance because he'd been running errands.

"Something wrong?" Elam asked.

"*Nein.* It's fine."

Legs wobbling, she forced another step. The porch faded behind her as she crossed the yard. She hesitated at the rear gate, her trembling hand hovering over the latch. The barn loomed in the distance, its silhouette heavy with dreadful memories.

Jaw tightening, she swallowed and forced herself to keep going.

I have to do this.

But her body betrayed her, every nerve screaming in protest. Pulse racing, her legs wobbled. The ground rippled, tilting as if it meant to swallow her whole. Objects crashed together, the sharp edges of the world dissolving into chaos.

She froze, unable to move. Her chest heaved as the air turned thick. "I can't—"

Panic surged, dragging her under. Desperate, she clawed at the space around her. Her knees buckled, and a sob tore from her throat as her vision blurred.

"Help," she gasped. "Don't let me fall…"

Chapter Three

Elam felt a jolt as Anika's fingers tightened around his hand. He wasn't sure what was happening, but the anxiety in her voice sent a chill down his spine.

"What's wrong?"

Anika shook her head, unable to answer. Her breath came in shallow, ragged gasps, and she squeezed his hand even tighter. The heat of her panic was a palpable tension vibrating in the air between them. A storm of fear swirled around her.

Elam glanced at her face, her eyes wide and unblinking, staring off into the distance as if the world around them had faded. Her lips quivered, the words she wanted to say stuck.

"Anika, what's going on?"

Her gaze flickered toward him. She swallowed hard, struggling to control her breath. "I—I—can't."

Thoughts spinning, he looked at the terrified girl. Was she having a seizure or some other sort of spell?

"I'll get help." But as he tried to free his hand, Anika's fingers tightened, a silent plea that stopped him dead in his tracks.

"*Nein*," she gasped. "Please—it's nothing. I just felt a little faint." She lifted a trembling hand to fan herself. "Like girls sometimes do."

Elam hesitated, studying her pale face. Ah. He had sisters. He understood.

"I'm fine," she insisted, her voice weak but insistent. "Give me a minute."

He wasn't convinced, but he saw the desperation in her eyes. Not just for him to believe her, but for him to drop it.

"If you say so," he relented, tightening his grip to steady her. "Let's sit on the porch. It's cooler there, and you can rest a minute."

She nodded. "*Ja.* That would be nice. *Danke.*"

Elam guided her back toward the house. The porch stretched wide and long, its wooden beams supporting a gently sloping roof that provided shelter from the sun. Vines crept up the posts and along the edges, their thick green tendrils weaving a natural curtain of leaves that offered dappled shade. The soft rustling of the leaves in the breeze added a peaceful ambience that provided a welcome escape from the warm afternoon.

As they walked, he felt the tension in her ease. She trusted him. At least for now.

Reaching the steps, he helped her settle down. "Okay if I sit?"

Anika glanced at the space beside her. "*Ja.*"

Elam lowered himself to the step next to her, keeping a respectful distance. He didn't want to crowd her or make her feel overwhelmed.

Just let her be.

He remained still, giving Anika the space she needed.

Taking a minute to study her features, he realized just how attractive she was. A delicate face was framed by tawny locks that had slipped loose from beneath her *kapp*. Her lashes were long, but it was her eyes that caught him most, deep brown with flecks of gold, like autumn sunlight filtering through the trees.

The silence stretched on. A long minute passed, and then another. The quiet of the afternoon wrapped around them, birds calling in the distance, the faint rustle of leaves in the breeze. The world felt muted, as though it had slowed down.

Anika straightened. "You must think I'm foolish acting this way."

Elam chuffed, trying to lighten the mood. "Not really. Wanna feel foolish? Because of what I did, I lost my license. Lost my job, too. Can't drive for a year."

Anika blinked, then let out a small, surprised laugh. "Seriously?"

"Yeah. The minute my boss heard, he fired me."

The tension around her mouth eased, her features softening. "I'm sorry."

Grimacing, Elam rubbed the back of his neck, the memory of it still fresh in his mind.

"I deserved it." Frustration flared, sharpening his tone. "Believe me, if I could take it all back, I would. I never meant to cause your family any harm. It just happened."

"Everyone messes up." Anika's gaze softened, more understanding now. "I'm sorry I was mean to you the other day. I know you didn't mean to hurt Nathan."

Elam blinked. Her sympathy was unexpected, and it left him feeling exposed in a way he hadn't felt before.

"I swear, it happened so fast that neither of us knew what happened."

"Nathan wasn't supposed to be out that late," she blurted. "*Daed* warned him not to go out on his bike after dark. He told him it was too dangerous, but he did it anyway."

"Sounds like we were all in the wrong place at the wrong time." His gaze drifted, focusing on nothing. He should have been home that night. But home… Home had nobody who cared if he was there or not.

Chest tightening, he fidgeted. He'd been born into a large brood—three older brothers and two sisters—yet somehow, he'd ended up the outsider. His parents were gone now, buried beside his grandparents in the small churchyard where generations of their kin rested. There was no one left to draw him back, no gentle reminder from *Mamm* to do better, no stern word from *Daed* to straighten his path. His brothers had their own households, their own farms and businesses, and his sisters lived busy lives filled with children and church gatherings.

Truth was, he was on his own. Ever since he'd stopped attending church, a subtle change had begun between himself and his brood. At first, it was just an absence—a Sunday morning here and there when he decided to stay home, or to go to work instead. But over time, that absence had grown, quietly, insidiously, until it had become a chasm.

I'm the one who decided to step away...

A gentle touch on his arm pulled him away from his thoughts.

"I didn't mean to make you feel bad," Anika said.

Swallowing, Elam forced a shrug. "It's not you. It's me. I've been so mad about the judge taking my license that I couldn't think about anything else. But the truth is, I did it to myself. I knew that street wasn't the place to race, but I let my pride get in the way. I wanted to shut Chris up. He's always bragging about his car and how it's unbeatable."

A beat of silence passed before Anika spoke, her voice barely above a whisper. "I caused a lot of problems, too...because I was mad."

Elam turned his head, uncertain if he'd heard her right. "What do you mean?"

Peeking over her shoulder to make sure they were alone, Anika leaned in closer. "I knew I wasn't supposed to do something, but I did it anyway."

His brows rose. "Oh?"

She hesitated, her fingers knotting into the folds of her apron. "I've been so scared." Voice faltering, she trembled, as if struggling to get the words out. "I think *Gott* is punishing me..."

Realizing what she was about to say, Anika pressed a trembling hand to her mouth. What in the world was she thinking?

The words perched on the tip of her tongue were more than just a passing thought. They were a confession. If she spoke them aloud, there would be no taking them back. They were a piece of the grief that had haunted her every waking moment since the day *Mamm* and Jason died.

Her throat tightened. She wasn't ready to say it. Not yet. Maybe not ever.

"I, um—" The words splintered into silence. A few days ago, she'd slammed the door in Elam's face without a second thought. Now, she was sitting beside him on the stoop, her heart hammering like a frightened bird, dangerously close to spilling everything.

How had it come to this?

We're not even friends.

The only reason Elam was here was that Bishop Graber had made him volunteer.

Not because he wanted to.

Because he had to.

Yet when she'd panicked, he hadn't pried. Hadn't demanded answers. He'd just sat beside her, steady and silent, waiting for her to find her breath again.

Elam didn't move. He sat with his elbows braced against his knees, his gaze fixed on the fields dotting the horizon. Maybe that's why she didn't immediately bolt back inside, why she'd lingered instead of shutting him out again. Not knowing him, she'd been quick to judge, an impulse born from her own fears. But his quiet strength made her hesitate. Something in his presence settled the turmoil inside her. He was easy to be with, and she liked that.

Ready to talk again, she exhaled slowly. "I used to be different."

Elam didn't react right away. He let the words settle, as if waiting to see if she would say more. When she didn't, he turned his head slightly. "Different? How?"

Anika hesitated. This was the moment to back out, to brush it off with some meaningless answer. But the fear and anxiety she'd buried for so long felt too heavy to keep inside.

"I wasn't always like this," she said, her voice barely above a whisper.

He didn't blink. "Like what?"

"Afraid."

"Why are you afraid?"

"Because of the accident," she confessed in a faint voice.

Elam nodded. "Losing people does that." His expression was shadowed. Knowing.

"You've lost someone, too." It wasn't a question.

He let out a breath. "Yeah, my parents. A car hit the buggy they were riding in."

A vague memory stirred from when she was younger. "I think I remember hearing about it."

"It was a long time before I could even think about getting back in one myself." His brow furrowed. "Truth be told, I still don't like to."

"Do you miss them?"

He nodded. "More than ever."

Anika's fingers brushed against his wrist before she pulled back. "I'm sorry."

Startled, Elam glanced down at where her hand had been, then back up at her. Something flickered in his gaze. "Me, too."

Needing to control her hands, she twisted them nervously in her lap. "Do you think *Gott* spares people pain when they die so awfully?" She wasn't sure why she had asked it, but the thought had been pressing on her mind ever since that terrible day.

"I haven't been to church in a long time," he confessed. "And I'm not sure what God thinks or plans. That said, I believe the Lord takes their spirits away quickly to spare them the pain." Leaning forward, his gaze drifted to the sky. "At least, I hope it's that way. That the end of this life is easy, and it isn't really the end at all."

"I'd like to believe that, too."

Elam ran a hand through his hair, disheveling it more than it already was. "It's what I think," he said. "But what I think and what I know don't always line up." Releasing a sigh, his shoulders slumped. "Bishop Graber's already had words with me. Smacked my hand for not coming to church. I reckon he's right, though." He glanced up, eyes meeting hers. "But I'm not sure how to settle it all in my mind yet."

Anika's heart twisted as her thoughts returned to what she'd meant to say when the conversation had begun. "I haven't gone to church in a long time, either," she confessed. "Not since everything happened."

"Why? If you don't mind me asking."

Anika trembled. The truth felt so heavy in her chest, but it was time. Time to face the shame she'd buried deep inside. "I'm scared *Gott*'s mad at me."

"Why would God be mad at you?"

Shame flooded her. "When I went on *rumspringa*, I wore makeup. And *Englisch* clothes."

He shrugged. "Plenty of Amish girls do that. It's all part of figuring out what the world's like, exploring things we can't do when we're living Plain. I don't think there's anything wrong with it."

"*Mamm* said I was disgracing her, showing so much skin and painting my face." Her voice faltered, the memory of their disappointment cutting deep. "When she found out, we fought. I told her—" Her words caught, but she forced herself to go on. "I told her I just wanted her to leave me be."

Once again, Elam didn't seem surprised. "I think every kid goes through that with their parents," he said. "I remember when I got my first cell phone. It was just a flip phone, nothing fancy. But I thought it was the greatest thing ever." He paused, shaking his head with a rueful smile. "I thought I had it hidden, too. Sure enough, my *mamm* found it."

"What did she do?"

"She took it and snapped it in half right in front of me. Said nothing like it would ever be in her *haus*. I was mad for weeks." He let out a long breath. "Still don't know how she found out about it. But she always had a way of figuring things out that I was trying to hide."

Anika nodded. "I could never keep anything from my *mamm*, either. No matter where I hid my stuff, she always seemed to know exactly where to find what I'd tucked away."

Elam laughed. "Parents are like that, I guess. It's their job."

A rush of fresh anguish suddenly filled her. "I didn't mean it when I said I wanted them to go away," she blurted. "I meant to say I was sorry, but I never had the chance."

"Because of the accident?"

"*Ja*. A few days later, the loft collapsed, and the bales fell." A single tear traced a path down her cheek. She brushed it away.

"That's awful," Elam murmured. "I remember Jason. He was a nice guy, always willing to help anyone in need."

Anika's gaze settled on the barn beyond the fence. After *Daed* lost his factory job, repairs fell by the wayside. The roof leaked, and every storm left its mark. Because of the economic downturn, most of their close relatives had moved on, starting over in other settlements. Not because they wanted to, but because they had to. Survival left little room for sentiment. But *Daed* had stayed. Too proud to ask for help, he clung to the farm and prayed steady work would return. Then one day, the weight of neglect came crashing down.

And nothing was ever the same.

"I didn't see what happened," she explained quietly. "But I heard the crash, and then the screams. When I rushed to the barn, I found them." Closing her eyes didn't banish the terrible images, but she tried. Desperately. Still, they lingered.

"And you think God's punishing you?"

Eyes brimming, Anika gasped. "*Ja.*" Her voice faltered, and she looked down at her hands, twisted tightly in her lap.

Elam leaned in. "God isn't punishing you," he said firmly. "It was an accident. A terrible accident."

A flicker of hope stirred. "You think so?"

"I know it," he said. "You're not the one to blame."

A fresh shiver ran through her. Frustrated, she clenched her fists. "I hate being this way—weak and afraid." How could she have any sort of future when the present felt so impossible to bear?

He didn't flinch. Instead, he sat there, solid and present. "Anyone can see you're doing the best you can."

Anika's breath hitched. "I've been trying," she whispered. "But it's been so hard."

Elam unexpectedly reached out. Not to pull her in. Not to console, but just to make contact. "I'll do what I can to help."

Accepting his touch, she didn't pull away. His hand on her shoulder was grounding. Real. It wasn't pity or obligation. Just a quiet assurance that someone saw her struggle.

"Promise?"

Gaze unwavering, he gave a firm nod. "Whatever it takes, I'll be here."

Chapter Four

"Thanks for the ride." Elam rubbed his stubbled face, glancing at the dashboard clock. Five thirty in the morning. No sane person should be up this early, but he had no choice if he wanted a ride.

Jace smirked, guiding his truck up the Glick farm's gravel drive. "Don't get too comfortable."

"Like I have a choice? Unless I can sprout wings, I'm stuck bumming rides." Elam yawned as Jace stopped near the gated fence. The Glick house, barn, and other outbuildings loomed in the predawn shadows.

"Is this your good deed for the day?" his friend teased. "Ready to shovel manure and haul hay?"

"That's the plan." Elam wasn't due until seven, so he had a few minutes to shake off the grogginess. Rolling out of bed this early wasn't ideal, but he wouldn't complain.

Jace raised a brow. "How's this work, anyway?"

Elam adjusted his ball cap, his hair recently cropped short for court. "The church has a program for guys like me—screwups who aren't total lost causes. Bishop Graber worked a deal with the judge. We help folks in the community, and it settles our debt."

"Sweet deal," Jace said. "Beats jail."

He rolled his eyes, grateful not to be sitting behind bars. "No kidding."

Jace frowned. "How'd you get that arrangement when Chris didn't? Thought you weren't Amish anymore."

Elam hesitated, staring out the window. "I didn't think so, either, but Bishop Graber convinced the judge this was better than lockup."

"So, you're Amish again?" Jace asked.

"I'm not sure." Elam gave a dry laugh. "All I know is I've got a hundred hours of work and time to think about it."

Jace leaned back, drumming the steering wheel. "You ever think about going back?"

"Sometimes," Elam admitted, bristling as the question hit deeper than expected. His life had been a whirlwind—mistakes he couldn't undo, choices he hadn't planned. Returning to the Amish felt like a tug-of-war between two versions of himself. "I don't have to decide today. I just want to finish this, fast."

Jace nodded, rolling down the window. "Sounds like a plan."

Elam glanced at his best buddy. Jace's curiosity wasn't prying; he just wanted to understand the Amish world, its rules, expectations, and struggles. "I'm not planning to go back. Don't know if I ever will."

"Got it," Jace said, sipping his coffee. "I need to head to work. We're hiring if you need something after your service."

"Flipping burgers?" Elam smirked.

"Pay's solid," Jace countered. "Evening shifts need hands. You'd make supervisor, easily."

Elam exhaled. His savings were nearly gone, swallowed by fines and attorney fees. "Nah. Not my scene. But thanks."

"Offer's open." Jace checked the time. "Catch you later?"

"I've got a ride home. Drop by when you get off and we'll play *Aetherfall Chronicles*." He snorted. "My army will crush yours."

Jace grinned. "We'll see." He eased the truck into gear, its taillights fading as he rumbled down the unpaved road.

Elam inhaled the crisp morning air, zipping his jacket. He

opened the gate and settled on the porch's wooden bench, its slats creaking. Pulling out his phone, he skimmed Bishop Graber's schedule: seven to nine at the farm. At ten, he'd head to the community center for a few more hours. After that, he'd be free. Maybe he'd take Jace's offer for evening shifts to rebuild his savings.

He couldn't ask his family for help. He'd already shamed the Mueller name enough. A tight knot formed in his chest. Community service wasn't just about serving time—it was about proving he wasn't the same fool who'd landed in trouble.

"Fix it and move on," he muttered, pocketing his phone.

The house was quiet, no lights on.

Leaning forward, Elam noticed the stillness of the predawn world. It felt peaceful, a calm he hadn't felt in years. He used to believe in all that. Church, prayer, the Word. Somewhere along the way, he'd stopped. Not out of defiance, just...no reason.

Did God still fit in a world of cell phones and satellites? The Bible spoke of burning bushes and miracles, but what about now? The answer should've been simple, but it wasn't.

Prayer had never come naturally. He had always skirted it, half-shamed by the thought of asking for anything, half-doubtful that anyone was listening. It seemed arrogant, even foolish, to bother the Lord with his troubles. So he'd remained silent, drifting further from the habit, the comfort.

Now, the absence of faith surged. His chest ached with longing, and shame tangled with hope. Could he dare to lift a voice he had silenced for so long? The question hovered, patient and persistent. He didn't know if he had the courage—or the words. But he wanted to try.

He pressed his palms together, hesitating. "Are You there, Lord? Or am I just talking to myself?"

Silence.

No warmth, no nudge. Just silence.

Restless, his fingers curled inward, clenching into fists. Maybe that wasn't how this worked. Maybe it never had.

He felt utterly alone. Abandoned.

And it was his own fault.

Night clung to the sky as Anika stirred awake, the house silent except for a faint breeze against the window. She groaned, rubbing her eyes, and pushed herself up. Her room was plain: a bed, a dresser, a shelf of worn books, a rag rug and handsewn curtains made from flour sacks. No mirror, no ornaments, just quiet necessity.

Striking a match, she lit an oil lamp, its flame flickering to life. Mornings had been brutal since the accident, reality stripping away the comfort of dreams where her mother and older brother still lived. Today, though, the dread felt lighter. Different.

The wind-up clock at her bedside read just shy of six. Soon, her father and Nathan would be up, and the day's demands would begin.

Pushing herself up, her bare feet met the cool floor. Wincing, she bent, slipping on her house shoes. The wooden boards creaked as she padded across her room. Nestled in the far corner, her washstand stood ready. A pitcher of water waited near the porcelain basin. Though the old house had a bathroom with indoor plumbing, she preferred dressing in the privacy of her room. Pouring out water, she dipped a cloth into the shallow depth.

Done, she slipped into the same old gray frock she wore daily. Her work apron, black leggings, and a pair of sturdy boots completed her outfit. Twisting her hair into a bun, she pinned her prayer *kapp* in place.

As she dressed, her gaze fell on the dusty Bible by her bed. She hadn't opened it, gripped by fear that *Gott* was punishing her for past disobedience. Guilt had made her feel unworthy of His comfort. But now, she understood. There was no hiding from *Gott*. He knew her remorse.

Reaching for the Bible, she opened to a marked passage: *Fear thou not; for I am with thee...*

A shaky breath escaped. It was exactly what she needed. Tears welled as she realized she'd turned away out of fear, yet *Gott* had never stopped waiting.

"*Danke*, Lord," she whispered, vowing not to let that distance grow again. Sitting down, she began to read.

"Anika, are you awake?" her father called, shattering the moment.

Anika started. She'd only meant to read for a minute. Somehow, half an hour had slipped away. Now *Daed* was up and needed help.

Closing the book, she rose and hurried to her father's room. She gave the door a light tap before entering.

Inside, her father gripped the lift bar mounted above his bed, his arms straining as he attempted to shift his weight. Face tight with concentration, he trembled with the effort of maneuvering himself into his wheelchair.

Anika hurried to his side. "Let me help."

Daed let out a breath. "I've got it."

Ignoring his pride, she placed one hand firmly on his back and the other on his forearm. "Just move to the left."

Readjusting his grip, *Daed* allowed her to brace him. Muscles strained, he moved himself sideways.

Once he was close enough, Anika guided his legs, ensuring they didn't tangle in the sheets. "You're almost there."

With a final push of effort, *Daed* lowered himself into his wheelchair. "Not as smooth as I'd like." He winced, rubbing one shoulder.

"You still did most of the work," she said. "Soon you'll be getting out of bed all by yourself."

"I want to be able to take care of things for myself." *Daed*'s voice was steady, but having to ask for help was a blow to his independence.

"Look how far you've gotten," she said, adjusting his footrests. "You're doing better every day."

Daed's lips pressed together. "I'm trying." His jaw tightened again. "With *Gott*'s help, I'll be out of this thing one day."

"I pray you will," she said, and reached for his robe.

Daed's lips twitched into a weary smile. "Guess I'd better start praying about it, then." He pointed toward the bedside. "Hand me my Bible, please. I'd like to spend a little time with the Lord while I wake up."

Anika retrieved the book and placed it in his hands. "I'll put the *kaffee* on." Leaving her father to his reading, she made her way back down the narrow hall.

Entering the kitchen, she snapped on the burners of the propane stove, the hissing sound filling the otherwise quiet space. The heat from the bright flames surrounded her like a comforting embrace. Moving to the sink, she rinsed yesterday's grounds out of the percolator's metal basket. A pile of dishes waited, too, but those weren't important.

A soft knock sounded at the front door.

Startled, Anika froze. The knock came again, quiet but insistent.

Her brow furrowed. She set the percolator down, wiping her hands on her apron as she made her way to the door.

"Elam?" she asked, surprised. "What are you doing here so early? Why, it's not even light yet."

Elam's gaze met hers with quiet intensity. "I didn't want to be late on my first day." He glanced toward the horizon, where the sun was just beginning to stretch over the edge. "Might as well get started, right?"

She hesitated. Dressed neatly in jeans, a T-shirt, boots, and a light jacket, his outfit looked effortlessly stylish. She couldn't imagine him wanting to ruin such nice clothes with the messy, labor-intensive tasks ahead. A shadow of stubble darkened his jaw, not enough to be untidy, just enough to give his features an edge.

"I guess," she said, stepping back to let him in. "Come on, then."

He stepped in. "Thanks."

The door clicked shut behind them. For a moment, neither of them moved. They simply stood there, caught in the discomfort of an unspoken tension.

Finally, Elam cleared his throat, "Just tell me what to do."

Anika had a lengthy list of tasks ahead, but the most pressing concern loomed. "Would you mind helping *Daed*? He still has difficulty getting washed and into his clothes. It's hard for him."

"You think he'd mind?" he asked. "I mean, I'm a stranger and that's kind of, uh, personal."

Memories of her father in the hospital flashed through her mind. Fragile and broken, he'd been surrounded by strangers tasked with helping him adjust to a life he hadn't chosen. Privacy had vanished. Dignity, too. In the end, he'd stopped resisting. Not because it got easier, but because he had no choice.

"He's used to people helping. He can still do some things on his own. Just step in when he needs it. Nathan usually handles it, but—" She opened her hands, the unfinished sentence hanging.

Understanding flickered. "Ah, okay. I can probably handle that."

Anika studied him. No pushback. No pause to think it over. He agreed without question, as if helping her was the most natural thing in the world.

Just like that, the problem had a solution.

An unexpected sense of optimism stirred in her chest. Maybe this could work.

At first, she'd dreaded the idea of having him around. She'd only agreed because Bishop Graber said it would help Elam fulfill the court's sentence. She hadn't seen much beyond that;

it had been just a requirement, a check mark on a list of things she had to endure.

Yesterday had changed that. When she'd melted with panic, Elam hadn't laughed or turned away. He hadn't stared at her like she was broken. Having lost his parents, he knew what it meant to wake up with immense grief and heartache.

Looking at him, her perspective suddenly changed. Yes, Elam had made mistakes. He'd caused trouble, no doubt. But hadn't *Gott* often worked through the flawed and imperfect to fulfill His will?

Setting aside her judgment, she decided to let a higher power lead the way.

If the Lord's willing to give him a chance, I should, too.

Chapter Five

"*Danke* for your help," Reuben Glick said. "I appreciate it."

Elam glanced up from where he knelt, rolling a sock over Reuben's foot. "Anytime."

Reuben exhaled, fingers curling against the armrest of his wheelchair. "I hate having to ask."

"Don't mention it," Elam replied, tugging the second sock into place and reaching for a boot. He guided Reuben's foot inside and tightened the laces.

Life changes fast, he thought. A large man, Reuben had once strode through life with strength and purpose. A cruel twist of fate had stolen that, leaving him bound to the wheelchair.

Elam swallowed, steadying himself. What must it be like to wake up unable to do what was once second nature? He'd hesitated when Anika asked him to help, not out of unwillingness but fear of clumsiness. If Reuben could bear needing help, he could offer it without faltering.

Reuben stared at his motionless feet. "It's hard getting used to this. I feel like a *boppli*."

Elam grabbed the second boot. "It's nothing. One more and we're done."

Reuben nodded. "I'm glad Bishop Graber sent you. Nathan helped, but with his leg broken, Anika had to step in. A *vater* should hold his daughter up, not the other way around."

Elam's hands stilled on the boot's strap. He heard the shame in Reuben's voice. "I don't think she sees it that way. Helping you makes her feel better."

"She's got a big heart, but taking care of me shouldn't be a daughter's burden." As if shamed, Reuben's gaze dropped. "She's not living anymore—just existing."

Elam recalled Anika's raw vulnerability yesterday, her brave face masking deep pain. "You've all been through a lot," he said. "It takes time."

Reuben shook his head. "I don't want her to sacrifice her future for me. She never finished her *rumspringa*. She should be looking ahead, building her own life."

"She's young," Elam said. "There's plenty of time for her to find herself."

Reuben sighed. "Youth passes quickly. I don't want her looking back with regrets."

"We'll get her out of the *haus*," Elam said, slipping into *Deitsch*. "You'll see her smile again."

Reuben's eyes brightened. "I'd be grateful for that." He gestured to the vanity. "Mind helping me shave? I'd like to comb my hair and trim my beard."

"Of course." Fetching the ceramic pitcher, Elam filled it with hot water from the bathroom. Back in the bedroom, he poured it into the basin and rolled Reuben's wheelchair closer. "Need a towel?"

Reuben nodded. "*Danke*."

Elam draped a towel over Reuben's shoulders, adjusting it carefully. "Good?"

"*Ja*, I can take it from here."

Reuben dipped a rag into the water, softening his stubble before reaching for his razor. "Hold the mirror, please."

Elam angled it for him. Reuben shaved with practiced ease, then trimmed his beard with small scissors.

Curiosity stirred. "What's it like? Being in a wheelchair?"

Reuben paused, staring at his reflection. "It's different. You accept it or fight it. I've had my time fighting."

"Was it easy to make peace with it?"

Reuben's jaw tightened. "*Nein.* I struggle with anger every day. Losing my *fraa* and *sohn* hurts more than this chair. But the Lord spared me. Like Job, I'll bear it and find purpose."

Elam stayed silent, struck by the older man's quiet strength.

Reuben wiped stray hairs from his face. "Didn't mean to get preachy. Sometimes the Lord stirs me."

"I don't mind listening." That part was true. Listening was easy. "Believing? Well, that's something else."

Reuben's eyes softened, filled with understanding. "Every man walks his own road to faith," he said. "Some find it early. Others, much later. One day, when you least expect it, *Gott* will take hold of you."

Unsure how to respond, Elam looked away. Something about Reuben's certainty scraped against his doubt.

Suddenly, he felt out of place, like a guest who'd overstayed his welcome at a gathering he hadn't meant to attend.

The morning sun filtered through the gingham curtains, casting a soft golden light across the worn wooden floor of the kitchen. It also illuminated the smudges on the windows and the dust clinging to the baseboards, a quiet rebuke of work left undone.

Anika frowned as she scrubbed a plate clean, the dishwater lukewarm and cloudy. She'd been so busy tending to the menfolk that the kitchen had slipped into untidiness. It pressed on her like everything else.

Ach, Mamm never would have let it get this way...

Frustrated, she set the plate in the drying rack with more force than necessary, then wrung out the dishcloth and turned to the table. She wiped it with firm strokes, determined to get the place back in order.

After the dishes came the broom. She swept crumbs from corners, dust from behind the stove, grit tracked in by boots too busy to stop. Then the mop—warm water, lye soap, the rhythm of back and forth. Her arms ached, but she didn't stop. Her list of chores stretched long, making her breath catch.

Whatsoever thy hand findeth to do, do it with thy might. The verse echoed in her mind, not as comfort, but as a challenge.

The thump of crutches broke her concentration.

"So, what do you think?" Nathan asked, grinning.

Anika glanced up from her sweeping. "About what?"

"Elam being here. You were madder than a wet hen the first time he showed up." Her brother shrugged, his thin shoulders rising and falling. "Figured you'd still be peeved."

She flicked a glance his way. "In retrospect, I may have misjudged the situation."

Nathan snickered. "Re-tro-spe-uct," he drawled, stretching the word out. "Sounds like you've been studying the dictionary again."

Anika narrowed her eyes at her younger brother, still in pajamas. "Unlike you, I enjoy learning new things. *Mamm* always said learning a new word each day keeps the mind sharp."

Nathan shrugged again. "Whatever. I've got better things to do than put my nose in a book."

"If you think you're going to sit around and play that video game I know you've got hidden from *Daed*, you'd better think again," she warned. "You're not going to weasel out while we do the work."

"We?" Nathan rolled his eyes. "Got a mouse in your pocket?"

"You know exactly what I mean," she shot back. "Elam and me."

His lips curled into a grin. "Sounds to me like you've gone all soft on Elam. 'Cos, you know, he's so tall and handsome." Puckering his lips, Nathan batted his eyelashes. "I bet you dreamed about kissing him last night, didn't you?"

Anika refused to be baited. She swiped the mop across the floor with hard strokes, as if she could scrub away his teasing. Even if the thought had crossed her mind, she'd never admit it. Elam was different—older, more experienced, and no longer rooted in Plain life. That alone put him far beyond her reach.

"Just leave me alone. I have work to do."

Sensing he'd pushed too far, Nathan eased up. "Where's he at?"

"Helping *Daed*." Anika kept sweeping. "You need to get dressed. There's a lot to do, and you're just dallying around."

Nathan sobered, balancing on his crutches. "I'll be glad when this cast comes off."

"Did the doctor say anything?"

"Another week, maybe two," he answered, glancing down. "I can't wait to get this thing off. I need to work on replacing my bike. Gotta earn the money for it first."

Anika sighed, softening. "We'll do our best," she promised. "You'll get that bike."

"Hope so," he said before heading to his room to get dressed.

As the door clicked shut, Anika frowned. Money was tight, and scraping together enough for anything new wouldn't be easy. But they'd figure it out. They always did.

She didn't hear the soft creak of floorboards until a voice broke the quiet.

"Hey," Elam said.

Startled, Anika turned. "Oh, hey. Is everything all right?"

"Yeah, fine. Got Reuben dressed and shaved."

"How is he?"

"He said he's feeling a little tired. Wanted to rest before breakfast."

Anika exhaled sharply, tension catching in her throat. "I've been so worried about that. He hasn't had much energy lately."

"I don't mean to pry," Elam said, choosing his words carefully, "but shouldn't he be getting some kind of physical therapy?"

"He's supposed to have it, but he won't go because we can't pay. And he won't apply for government aid, either."

"Seems any help would be better than none."

"That's just the way *Daed* is." Her voice trembled. "He's worked his whole life. Now that he can't, he feels like a burden."

"I get that," Elam said. "I don't know if I could handle living my life in a wheelchair."

"*Daed*'s struggling," she admitted. "But he's always had a powerful faith. Even through everything, he's the one holding us together." She glanced down, her voice softer. "If anyone's weak, it's me. I'm the one who turned away from *Gott*."

"Don't be so hard on yourself. You've been through a lot, trying to hold things together. That takes strength, too."

Anika stilled. His words hit deep. The constant weight of holding everything up had become so normal, it no longer felt like a feat. "I never saw it that way."

Elam gave her a long look. "That's exactly what it is. Strength. You kept going, even when you were scared. That's not just strong. That's brave."

"You think so?"

"I don't think it. I know it."

A brief silence stretched between them, charged with something fragile and new.

Nervous, Anika brushed a hand down her apron to smooth it. "Have you had anything to eat?"

Elam shook his head. "Didn't have time. Had to get up early to catch a ride."

She glanced at the clock. An hour had slipped away, and breakfast wasn't started. Scrambled eggs, bacon and toast would have to do. "I'd better fix something before *Daed* and Nathan start making a fuss," she said. "Would you care for a cup of *kaffee* while I cook?"

"Sure." His smile deepened. "Thanks for asking."

Anika reached for the canister of *kaffee* beans. The rich, earthy scent rose as she pried off the lid.

"Let me," Elam said, stepping up. He moved with easy grace.

"*Danke*," she said, handing over the tin.

Their fingers brushed, and a spark of static crackled between them.

He laughed. "You're more electrifying than I thought."

Anika's lips curved into a small smile. "I've never been so shocked." She cringed, realizing how cheesy that sounded.

Gaze lighting up, Elam's grin widened. "And I'm simply charged with anticipation," he returned, continuing the puns.

She rolled her eyes. "Keep this up and you'll short-circuit me."

"Is that a warning or a promise?" he teased, stepping closer.

His nearness stole her breath. "Um… It's n-neither," she stammered, retreating to the cold box. Grateful for the distraction, she pulled out the eggs, milk and butter, then reached for the cast-iron skillet hanging on its hook. Familiar movements grounded her—cracking eggs into a bowl, adding a pinch of salt and pepper, whisking until the yolks and whites blurred into golden silk. The rhythm steadied her hands, calming the flutter inside.

"Haven't had fresh ground in a long time," he commented, tending his task. "Always just throw a teaspoon of instant into a cup."

"Then you're in for a treat," she said, glancing over her shoulder. "But don't mill the beans too fine."

He chuckled. "Hard to mess up turning a handle."

"Maybe," she said. "But *Daed* always grinds them down. Says he likes it strong."

Elam kept going. "I like a strong cup myself. Hot, black and plain."

Anika grimaced. "Guess I'm a sissy. I like cream and sugar in mine."

"Nothing wrong with a little sweet." He winked. "It helps chase away the bitter."

His teasing touched a soft spot, the part of her that missed laughter and being with someone special.

He's not that bad.

Days ago, the thought of having Elam around had set her teeth on edge. Now, here he was. Not by accident, but by invitation. They'd needed help, and the hands had been provided.

Maybe a greater power really was working. Not with flashes of lightning and fiery brimstone, but in gentler, more deliberate ways.

A hush settled over her, a fragile, precious calm. The mountain of chores still loomed, each task demanding more than two hands could manage. Yet somehow, with Elam working quietly beside her, it didn't feel quite so impossible. For the first time in a long while, she felt something she thought she'd lost.

Hope.

Chapter Six

Elam leaned back in his chair, a satisfied groan escaping as he pushed his plate away.

"I can't eat another bite."

"Are you sure?" Anika lifted the platter, offering more bacon. "There's plenty."

"I'm stuffed," he said, folding his napkin. "One more bite and I'll pop."

Across the table, Reuben let out a hearty laugh. "Anika learned to cook from her *mamm*. There's nothing she can't make."

Anika began gathering the dirty dishes, stacking them in the sink before running hot water into the basin. "Well, right now I need to make these dishes disappear."

Elam rose. "I should get up and work off some of this meal. Just tell me what to do and I will."

"I'll show you what needs to be done," Nathan said, reaching for his crutches.

"That would be great. Thanks."

"Let me wash up." Nathan pushed himself to his feet. "I'll be right there." Sliding the crutches beneath his arms, he steadied himself before making his way toward the bathroom, his movements deliberate but determined. The soft thud of rubber tips against the wooden floor faded as he disappeared down the hall.

Reuben drained the last of his *kaffee* before rolling himself away from the table. "Much as I'd like to dally, I've got work of my own." Awkwardly turning his wheelchair, he maneuvered into the living room. He stopped beside a table where blocks of wood and a well-worn whittling knife waited. "These carvings won't finish themselves."

Anika moved to collect the empty cup. "*Daed* likes to keep busy," she murmured, her voice carrying a note of quiet affection.

Elam tucked away the information, filing it alongside the dozen other small observations he'd gathered. Since stepping into the house, he'd been drawn into the quiet rhythm of their lives. It was disorienting. The casual warmth unsettled him, pressing in on all sides.

"I'll wait for Nathan outside," he said, heading toward the door, the fresh air beyond promising a moment of solitude before the work began.

"I'll send him out," Anika said, returning to her dishes.

Walking outside, Elam closed the door behind him. Looking around, he couldn't fail to notice that most of the buildings had seen better days. Beyond the back fence, livestock pens stretched out in modest disarray, a scattering of wooden enclosures. The scents of hay, mud and the faint musk of manure lingered in the air. A pair of milk cows occupied the far paddock, their presence a reminder of the life sustained here. Not for profit, but for the family's simple needs.

His gaze drifted to the barn where the accident had occurred. Recent repairs couldn't entirely mask the weathered lines etched through the years. The silent signs of hardship were there, easy to see if one looked close enough.

The Glicks were struggling. Though the property was only a few acres in size, the loss of working hands had left more labor than a few people could reasonably manage.

There's so much to do.

His mind reeled back to the day before, when Anika had broken down right in this very spot. Recalling how she'd faltered, he felt shame crash over him. Losing her *mamm* and *bruder* was devastating. Her father, now handicapped, was unable to provide. His careless actions had hurt her younger brother, too, stripping away yet another pillar of support she desperately needed.

He hadn't truly understood before how one negligent choice could ripple outward, altering lives in ways he never intended. But now, it settled deep in his conscience. He realized then that people's lives were woven together. That was the essence of community. Each person was a thread in the whole, their fates all bound together. In harming another, he'd frayed those threads.

You're such a bonehead, he thought, chastising himself. *Do better.*

The creak of old hinges broke through his thoughts, the sound carrying in the stillness of the morning.

Expecting Nathan to join him, Elam turned. But it wasn't Nathan. It was Anika.

Stepping out, she squinted against the pale light of the sun. Her hands were raw and chapped, red from the hot water she'd used to scrub the dishes.

"Everything okay?" he asked.

She hesitated, then nodded. "*Ja.* Fine." She tucked a stray lock of hair behind her ear, then managed a small, tentative smile. "I just wanted to thank you for helping *Daed.*"

He shook his head dismissively. "It's nothing."

"You're wrong," she said. "To me, it's something."

That caught his attention. He studied her, curiosity stirring. "Oh? How so?"

Fidgeting, Anika pressed her lips together. Then, as if the words had been waiting to burst free, she blurted, "I didn't think you'd be very nice about having to help out here."

Elam blinked, attempting to mask the awkwardness coiling tight in his chest. He hadn't realized he had a reputation that preceded him, much less one that made people brace for the worst.

"I try to be decent." And he meant it. The last thing he

wanted was to be remembered for the mistakes he'd made, yet it seemed like that's all anyone could see.

Anika studied him. "I mean, when you showed up that day, I had this whole picture in my head of what you'd be like. And you're...not that."

Elam chuckled. If that was a compliment, he'd take it. "I'm trying," he said. "Not to be so wrapped up in myself." He let out a breath. "I can't undo what I've done. All I can do now is try and be better." He shook his head. "The judge called this my chance. I'm trying not to waste it."

Stepping closer, Anika cocked her head. "Now that I've gotten to know you, I kind of like you."

"Yeah?"

She shrugged, the motion light but with a hint of playfulness. "Yeah."

"I kind of like you, too." He paused, then added, "If you'll give me a chance, I hope we can be friends."

Anika's smile faltered, uncertainty flickering in her gaze. But then, just as quickly, her hesitation gave way to something hopeful.

"That would be nice." As she spoke, the sun's light cast a warm glow on her face, catching the golden undertones in the curls that escaped her *kapp*. In that moment, she was breathtaking.

Elam gulped. He wasn't supposed to notice things like that. But he did. He had, from the first time he saw her.

The thump of crutches disrupted the quiet moment.

Elam turned just as Nathan emerged, moving toward them with measured steps. Hat on his head, he was dressed for work, his sleeves rolled up. But it was his gaze that held weight. Sharp, assessing and spanning the narrow space between them.

"Everything all right?"

Elam fought back a smile. If it had been his sister standing there with a man of questionable reputation, he'd have felt the same way.

Shoving his hands into his pockets, he gave a casual nod. "We were just talking."

Anika took a quick step back. "Nothing's going on."

Nathan smirked, the kind of grin only an annoying little brother could perfect. "Didn't say it was." His gaze flicked toward the barn. "Animals need tending." He shifted his weight on his crutches before looking at Elam. "I'll show you where everything is."

Elam studied the youth's lanky frame. Nathan should have been a carefree teenager, still clinging to those last precious years before adulthood came crashing in. Instead, he was carrying a man's responsibilities, keeping the work going, looking out for his sister, all while balancing on crutches.

"Lead the way," he invited.

Anika lifted her chin, a spark of determination flashing in her eyes. "I'll go, too."

Concern lifted Nathan's brows. "You sure?"

She hesitated a beat before nodding. "*Ja.* I am."

"All righty, then," Nathan said. "We've got a lot to do." With that, he led the way, his crutches stamping against the ground.

Anika hesitated a fraction of a second before stepping forward. "Let's go."

Elam fell into step beside the two siblings. If Anika faltered, he'd be there.

The barn loomed ahead, its weathered wooden frame stark beneath the morning light. To anyone else, it was just a building. But from Anika's point of view, it was more than that.

It was a graveyard.

Reaching the barn's entrance, Anika stopped short. Stepping inside meant facing everything she feared…everything waiting for her in the shadows.

Nathan stood beside her, gripping his crutches tightly, his

posture rigid with unspoken words. Though only fourteen, his face carried the weariness of someone much older.

Beside him, Elam stood staunchly, his presence steady and unshaken.

"You don't have to do this," Nathan murmured.

"I do," she insisted, shivering. "I have to."

Elam straightened, his keen gaze settling on her. "We'll be with you. Every step."

Anika swallowed, nodding. Steeling her resolve, she stepped forward. The barn's interior loomed before her, dim and uninviting. The sharp tang of straw mixed with the earthy musk of leather and wood invaded her nostrils. Locked in their stalls, the horses snorted and shuffled.

She paused. The entire space was familiar, unchanged, yet everything about it felt different. Life for some had gone on here, even when for others it had stopped.

"You okay?" Nathan asked.

Anika pulled a breath. "*Ja.*" Everything looked fine. Normal. The loft had been rebuilt, and the wagon stood as it always had. Her favorite horse shifted restlessly.

"Hey there, Mossie," she murmured, using the nickname she'd called the mare since she was a wobbly-legged foal.

The horse's ears flicked toward her. A nicker of recognition followed.

Approaching the stall, Anika reached out and ran her hand along the mare's head. "I missed you." She'd raised the horse herself, watching her grow from a fragile, spindly thing into the strong, dependable animal standing before her now. Broad-backed and patient, Mossie was more than just a companion; she was a cornerstone of farm life.

"Been a long time since we've gone anywhere," she whispered, remembering the days when the sun hung high and warm. Chores done, she'd hitch up the wagon and head out for hours, the world stretching out before her, full of possibility.

But now, standing in this space, the past pressed down, heavy and unyielding.

Giving the mare a final stroke, she turned away.

She'd come here to remember, to find some kind of peace. But the more she looked around, the more it seemed out of reach.

And then it happened. A sudden searing heat flashed over her, turning her limbs to lead. Memories surged, vivid as the day they'd been etched into her life.

Trembling, she let them come, refusing to push them away.

The morning had opened cool and crisp, the kind of air that told you autumn had finally started to settle across the land. Having made a trip to town, *Daed*, *Mamm* and Jason had pulled the wagon, filled to the brim with hay and other supplies, into the barn to unload it.

Seeing them arrive, Anika had waved but didn't join them. Busy tending her chores, she was hanging the freshly washed clothes on the line. Then came the crash. A terrible, splintering crack, followed by a cacophony of screams. And then there was silence as disaster swallowed everything.

The last piece of clothing had slipped from her hands as she ran, her feet barely touching the ground. Heart in her mouth, she burst into the barn. Immediately, she knew what had happened. The upper loft had given way, collapsing in a choking storm of dust and other debris. Bales of hay, so deceptively soft in appearance, had come crashing down with brutal force, burying her family beneath a crushing weight.

For a moment, she'd frozen, her breath coming in short, panicked gasps. Then instinct had taken over. Throwing herself at the bales, she'd fought to shift them, clawing at the mass with shaking hands.

But the bales wouldn't move. They were too heavy. Too many. The farm had no phone. No way to call for assistance. The barn, once a place of warmth and shelter, had become a place of disaster and death.

Nathan had finally arrived from his errands to find them all there, helpless beneath the fallen weight of wood and hay. He was the hero of the day. He'd gone for help.

And I did nothing...

In the days after the accident, the world blurred into a stream of casseroles, condolences and whispered prayers. The double funeral had come and gone in a haze of black outfits and stiff embraces, the cold earth swallowing two more pieces of her heart. *Daed* couldn't attend. His body was too broken, confined to a hospital bed miles away.

Anika had stood in his place, quiet and composed, making the arrangements, accepting the neighbors' kindness with a nod. She moved like a machine, efficient and numb, as if holding everything together by sheer will alone.

And then, one morning, she fell apart.

It had started with a breath that wouldn't come, a tightness in her chest that turned into trembling hands and a rising terror that made no sense. Her knees gave out as the world spun and her heart galloped wildly. That first panic attack cracked something open, and after that, everything unraveled. Her life, once full of rhythm and purpose, came to a screeching halt.

She gasped as the edges of her vision warped, blurring everything around her. The ground beneath her tilted, shifting as though the whole planet had flipped itself upside down.

She staggered, one step, and then another. "No..." Breath hitching, her knees buckled. The ground rushed up to meet her.

At the last second, Elam stopped her fall. "I've got you." Grip firm and sure, his steady presence was a solid anchor. Holding her gently, he kept her on her feet.

"Get me out," she gasped, leaning against him.

"Take deep breaths," he advised. "It'll clear your head." Guiding her outside, he nudged her toward a bench tucked beneath the overhanging eaves. As he lowered her to sit, his hands lingered on her shoulders, a gentle pressure as though to steady her, not just physically but emotionally.

"*Danke*," she whispered, releasing a long, grateful sigh.

Nathan followed, his crutches thudding against the ground. "Are you okay?"

"I think so." She blinked, trying to clear the haze clouding her vision. "I just need some air."

Elam studied her with quiet concern. "You had us worried for a minute."

"It all came back so fast." She let out a shaky laugh. "It's strange, but it looks like none of it ever happened. Like it wasn't real."

It was true. Thanks to the dedicated hands of volunteers, the loft's unstable beams had been replaced with fresh, solid lumber. Completely restored, it easily held the stacked bales. But everything about it felt off. Despite the repairs, the aftermath lingered.

"Things were fixed," Nathan said. "That's how it's meant to be. Even the Bible talks about it. Remember when Jerusalem was burned? Nehemiah led the rebuilding so it would no longer be a place of despair."

Anika's gaze dropped, her breath shallow, her hands trembling. Everything looked normal, but it felt like a mirage.

"I don't know what's wrong with me." Frustrated, she clenched her fists. "Why can't I be better?"

Elam leaned close. "Don't be so hard on yourself. Look how far you got."

"First time you've been past the back gate in a long time," Nathan added, his voice full of encouragement. "I didn't think you could, but you did."

"Then why do I feel so stupid and weak?" she mumbled, swiping at teary eyes.

"You're not weak," Nathan countered. "You're just trying to work things out, that's all."

Anika sat, desperately trying to distract herself from the ache threatening to smother her. But it didn't help. Nothing ever did. How could she look forward to the future when she was too afraid to live in the present?

"I think you've had enough," Elam said. "Nathan and I can handle things now."

"*Ja*," her brother agreed. "We got this."

Giving both a grateful look, Anika pushed herself up from the bench. "I have a lot to do," she said, brushing damp palms against her apron. Her legs were unsteady, but she held her ground. "Sitting around like this is just wasting time."

"Nothing was wasted," Elam said. "You did fine."

Anika didn't wait for more. "I guess." Turning away, she hurried back toward the house. Each step felt like lead.

That's when it hit her and sank in. She wasn't being brave. She was running away. Again. Fleeing like a spooked rabbit.

No more. I've had enough.

If she wanted to heal, she had to move forward. Not just physically, but inwardly. She had to show up for herself. Even when it hurt. Especially when it hurt.

Reaching the safety of the gate, she held on to the thought like a lifeline. She'd made it this far. Out the back door and past the back fence, going all the way to the barn. She'd even stepped inside, daring to face the demons she'd spent so long avoiding.

Now that she had, she'd keep going. Keep showing up until fear was crowded out.

And she would pray.

Not the soft, half-hearted kind that came in a whisper of uncertainty, but the kind that came from her gut, the hollow center of her very soul.

She wasn't healed. Not yet.

But she was determined to take the first steps toward it.

Chapter Seven

Elam stood in the barn doorway, one arm braced against the wooden frame, the other hanging limp at his side. Sweaty and hot, his shirt clung to his skin. Mud and other gunk streaked his jeans, and his boots were covered with something smelly.

"Gross." He hadn't worked this hard in years. Hauling wrecked cars was a breeze compared to toiling on a working farm.

Nearby, Nathan leaned into his crutches. "Just wait till we get to the pigpens," he joked. "That's where the real dirty work comes in."

"Oh, great," Elam groaned as memories of the morning's tasks filtered back, each leaving a dull ache in his shoulders. The Glick place wasn't large, but it demanded more than its share of labor to keep the people and animals fed and thriving. He'd done as much as he could, hauling water and feed to the livestock before moving on to mucking out the horse stalls. After pitching what felt like a ton of hay, he'd tackled a few repairs on the chicken coops, including a broken latch that had been letting the hens wander.

"Oh, we haven't even gotten started," Nathan said, rolling his eyes. "Don't forget, the rabbit pens need to be raked out, too."

"Seriously?" Though the hours had flown by, he'd never realized how much there was to do and how the loss of capable hands could bring the whole operation to a crawl.

Nathan nodded. "Yep."

"Can't say I'm looking forward to it." Might as well be honest. Dealing with manure wasn't his favorite way to spend the day. It was a reminder that growing up in the countryside and growing up on a farm were two very different things. His mother had gardened for pleasure. These people planted gardens because they needed to eat.

There was a lot to be done, and he should have shown up a lot sooner than he had. But he'd been too wrapped up in his problems to care what others were going through. It wasn't until after his sentencing that he finally reached out to the Glick family. Unaware of their losses, he hadn't understood how much Nathan's accident had cost them. Things they couldn't afford to lose, things he hadn't even thought to consider. The damages he'd contributed to weren't abstract anymore. Now that he'd arrived, he saw the harm he'd inflicted had people with faces. People with names. People with needs.

Once again, the divide between those who had plenty and those who scraped by felt sharper than ever. He hadn't grown up poor. He'd never gone without.

Don't know how they manage.

But they did. With grit, prayer and a kind of quiet determination he hadn't realized existed.

The creak of the back gate cut through his thoughts.

Across the way, Anika emerged onto the wagon path between the house and the barn, moving with measured steps as she balanced a tray in both hands.

"I thought you could use a break," she said, holding up a tray with tall glasses of iced lemonade.

Elam swiped a hand across his face as she approached. "You're officially my favorite person," he said, gratefully accepting the glass she offered. "I was about to thirst to death." He took a long drink. The lemonade was cold, refreshingly tart.

Anika gave the barn a wary look. "Why don't we sit over there?" She nodded toward a picnic table tucked beneath a cluster of trees. Tall and stately, their extended branches provided a welcome canopy. "It's cooler in the shade."

"I could use a break," he agreed, moving toward the table. At the soft crunch of gravel behind him, he paused and turned. Nathan was making his way across the uneven surface, his crutches biting into the ground. Perspiration trickled down his temples despite the brim of his straw hat.

"Be glad when these are gone."

Elam slowed. "Almost there."

"Not soon enough," Nathan grumbled. While he'd done his best to help, the crutches limited what he was able to do. Handling a pitchfork or a wheelbarrow was almost impossible when both hands were tied up maneuvering two long wooden sticks.

Regretting the damage he'd done, Elam momentarily flashed back to that night: the screech of tires, the crunch of metal, the stunned silence that followed. The way Nathan had lain on the pavement, half-crumpled and writhing in pain, was something he'd never forget.

"When's that cast coming off?"

"Soon," Nathan said, his tone brightening. "Doctor says my leg is healing well."

"That's great."

The trio settled into the quiet of the shade, enjoying the welcome relief from the rising heat.

Elam took another drink. "That hits the spot." Sighing in appreciation, he leaned back. "Thanks."

"Lunch will be ready soon," Anika said, tucking a strand of hair behind her ear. "Nothing fancy, just sandwiches. I made cookies, too. Oatmeal, with pecans and raisins."

"Sounds good," he said. "But I can't stay."

"Oh?"

Elam fished his cell phone out of his back pocket to check the alarm he'd set. "Yeah. Bishop Graber kind of volunteered me for something."

"Doing what?" Nathan asked.

"I'll be helping to pack meals for the folks in town who can't get around much anymore," he explained, slipping the phone back into his pocket. "You know, people who'd go hungry otherwise."

Anika's eyes lit up. "*Mamm* used to volunteer," she said. "I used to go, too."

"We all used to," Nathan added. "Jason wanted to learn to drive so he could do more."

"Is that right?" Elam asked, leaning forward.

"*Mamm* said absolutely not," Anika cut in, her face darkening with concern.

"*Mamm* always said no to anything *Englisch*," Nathan countered. "But *Daed* said if he thought he was mature enough, he could make his own choices. That's the way of it. If you're not baptized, you're free to do what you want."

Anika's expression turned solemn. "Sometimes doing what you want isn't the right thing," she scolded. "The Lord says there will be woe to the obstinate children. I believe that. With all my heart. We can't just run ahead of *Gott* because we're chasing what we think we want."

Aware that the bishop would arrive any minute, Elam set his glass aside. "Didn't expect to get this dirty," he muttered, brushing at the grime on his clothes.

"You can't handle food stinking like that," Anika exclaimed, frowning with disapproval.

Elam spread his hands. "You're right. But I don't have anything else to wear."

Nathan studied him for a moment. "You're about Jason's size. You could borrow something of his."

Anika froze.

Elam saw the way her shoulders tensed, how her mouth pressed into a tight line. Guilt curled in his stomach. "I don't think that's a good idea."

Nathan didn't waver. "But Jason's clothes are still in his room. They should fit, so why not loan them out?"

Anika crossed her arms over her chest. "Nathan, please stop..."

"It's okay," Nathan insisted before turning toward his sister. "*Daed* said he wanted to donate them, but no one's ever gotten it done."

Anika's fingers fidgeted with the hem of her apron. "I couldn't pack up his things," she admitted. "I know I should, but I...can't."

"There's no reason to let things sit when someone else can use them," Nathan said.

Unwilling to let the argument escalate, Elam raised his hands. "It's no big deal," he said, signaling for a truce. "I'll borrow your washroom and clean up the best I can."

"It wouldn't be proper to show up like that," Anika said, again eyeing his soiled clothes.

"I'm sure we can find a shirt and some trousers," Nathan added, gathering his crutches. Taking a few steps, he looked back toward the stragglers. "You all coming?"

Anika reluctantly stood. "I suppose he wouldn't mind." Gathering the empty glasses, she returned them to the tray.

Elam hesitated. "If it hurts you too bad—"

"I'm fine," she insisted, her tone soft but resolute.

Then he saw it. Not just the steadiness in her eyes, but the quiet courage behind them. Her strength wasn't just in her ability to carry on. It was in the way she kept pressing forward, even when she was afraid.

They barely knew each other. But something about her stuck. Maybe it was the way she met his eyes without flinching. Maybe it was just that she kept going, even when it hurt.

She noticed him watching. A little color crept into her cheeks. "Something wrong?"

He rose. "Just thinking."

She tilted her head. "About what?"

Elam's pulse quickened. "Nothing important."

But it wasn't nothing.

It was something.

He just didn't know what to do with it yet.

Standing at the threshold of her brother's room, Anika rested her hand on the latch. She hadn't opened the door since the day he'd died. The silence his absence had left in their lives was deeper than the one that filled this room now. No songs drifted down the hallway. No laughter or sounds of the banjo he used to play. Just the aching hush of nothing.

He's not coming back.

So here she was. She had to go inside, get the clothes. Elam needed a clean shirt and trousers.

Bracing herself, she pushed the door wider. It creaked on its hinges, as if reluctant to let her in. The hush of stillness greeted her. Curtains half-drawn, cobwebs hung in the corners like neglected threads of memory.

She looked around. Everything was just as Jason had left it. His work boots sat beneath the window, and his favorite denim jacket was draped over a rocking chair. The Bible he'd cherished rested open on the nightstand. Handwritten notes marked the last passages he'd read.

Anika stepped inside, her heels making a hollow sound on the wooden floor. Her fingers brushed the back of the chair as she walked toward the dresser. She hesitated before opening it.

She stared at the neatly folded shirts, her hand hovering over a blue cotton one. Slowly, she picked it up, smoothing the fabric between her fingers.

This looks like it will fit.

Her throat tightened. Opening another drawer, she picked out a pair of plain black trousers. She'd need to find a pair of suspenders, too. Without them, the britches wouldn't stay up properly.

Gathering what she needed, she turned to leave. Her gaze was drawn to the banjo propped in the corner. A simple thing, but full of memories for the hours of entertainment it had given. Jason had been a musician, and he'd dreamed of starting a Christian band.

Mamm had never approved. Said music was for worship, not entertainment. But Jason had played anyway. While most Old Order communities shunned musical instruments, some of the more progressive groups made quiet allowances. On Sunday, they'd bring them out to play.

Bishop Graber was also wise enough not to forbid it. He understood that young people needed joy, too. If having a little hoedown gave them that, it was better to look the other way than to shut the door entirely.

Picking up the banjo, Anika sat on the bed. She didn't know the first thing about playing, but she remembered Jason's fingers picking over the strings. She strummed a few chords, out of tune and clumsy, but the sound was warm. Familiar.

She smiled through the sting in her eyes. "I wish you'd taught me," she whispered. "Maybe I'll learn. Someday."

A voice down the hall broke through the hush of the moment.

"Anika?" *Daed* called.

Startled, she jumped off the bed. Setting the banjo back in its corner, she grabbed the clothes. Taking one last glance around the room, she hurried out. The door clicked shut behind her. Later, she would come back. Later, she would pack Jason's things.

Later.

Elam waited in the living room, visiting with *Daed* and Nathan. All three looked up as she entered.

"Did you find something?" *Daed* asked.

Anika showed what she'd selected. "*Ja.* I think these will fit."

"Thank you for letting me borrow them," Elam said, accepting her offering. "Mind if I use your washroom?"

"Help yourself," *Daed* invited.

"I'll just be a minute," Elam said, heading down the hall.

Anika watched him go, her gaze following the set of his shoulders. Then he disappeared down the hall, shutting the door behind him. The sound of running water soon followed.

She turned away, cheeks flushed with heat she couldn't explain. "I hope they fit," she said, uncertain about her feelings. How would it feel, seeing someone else wearing her brother's clothes?

Daed glanced at her with a soft look in his eyes. "It's all right," he soothed. "Jason would want them to be worn. Better for them to serve some purpose than rot away in drawers."

"I know that's the way it should be."

"But?"

"It feels wrong that we've gotten to go on with our lives—" A sudden gasp tore out. "—and *Mamm* and Jason haven't."

"Going on with our lives doesn't mean we've done anything wrong, either," *Daed* said.

Anguish twisted hard. "Then why does it feel that way?"

Rolling his wheelchair closer, her father took her hand. "Because grief tricks you into thinking you have to hold on to pain to keep their memory alive. But that's not true. Letting yourself heal doesn't mean you're leaving them behind. It means you're carrying them with you, just in a different way."

Emotion tightened her throat. "I don't know how."

Daed offered a smile. "You don't have to figure it all out today. But you're not alone. You have me, and Nathan, and so many others who love you."

"That's true," Nathan added. "We'll always have each other."

Anika nodded, but her emotions still felt tangled up.

A heavy knock at the front door indicated a visitor had arrived.

Anika hurried to open the door. Bishop Graber stood on the porch, broad hat in hand, his silver hair catching the sunlight.

"*Guten morgen*," he greeted with a warm smile.

"Bishop," she replied, stepping aside. "Come in."

Nodding his thanks, James Graber entered, offering a greeting to the others. "Hello, Reuben. I hope the day finds you well." He glanced toward Nathan and added, "And you, too, Nathan." He looked around for another face. "I don't see Elam."

"He's washing up," Nathan explained. "He mucked out the stalls earlier and needed a change. We lent him some of Jason's clothes. He'll be out in a minute, I'm sure."

"Makes sense," Bishop Graber chuckled. "I know how that goes."

Daed wheeled forward to shake the church elder's hand. "What brings you by?"

"I'm here to pick up Elam," the bishop explained. "He'll be helping with the meals program."

Daed's face lit up. "I remember how much Ada loved cooking for that."

"Everyone still talks about her beef stew," the bishop said, his smile softening. "Best anyone ever made, if you ask me."

"*Danke*," *Daed* laughed. "Ada would appreciate your kind words."

Bishop Graber smiled back. "I mean them, sincerely and absolutely. She was a fine cook." Then he turned to Anika. "Do you still make those shortbread cookies? I remember how everyone enjoyed the treat so much."

"*Nein*," she said. "I haven't made any since *Mamm* passed."

The bishop tsked. "That's too bad. I always thought you made the best desserts for the potlucks after church." Pausing, he added, "Been quite a while now since you've gone."

Anika swallowed hard. "I suppose it has."

Bishop Graber settled into a chair, gesturing for her to do the same. "I haven't had the chance to visit with you much," he said. "How are you holding up?"

Anika lowered herself to sit, folding her hands in her lap. "I'm managing."

"And how are things going with Elam?"

She shook her head. "Elam's fine. I have no problem with him."

"That's encouraging."

"Anika's doing better," Nathan added. "This morning, she went into the barn."

Bishop Graber gave a thoughtful nod. "How did that make you feel?"

Anika glanced at her hands. "I was scared. I almost turned around before I went inside. But I told myself I didn't have to do anything. Just go inside. And I did."

Compassion softened the church elder's expression. "You've shown great courage. Sometimes the smallest steps are the hardest to take."

"Do you think I'll ever get better?"

A kind smile touched his lips. "When I am afraid, I put my trust in *Gott*. Sometimes going forward means trusting the Lord is fighting the battle while you take the next step. Remember, even when you're scared, you are never alone. He will see you through." Reaching out, he gave her hand a light squeeze. "Just give it a try. It works, I promise."

Calm determination settled over her. "I'm going to."

Before the conversation could progress, the washroom door creaked open.

Elam walked into the living room. "Sorry to keep you waiting," he said, seeing the bishop.

"I've no worry," James Graber replied.

Anika's breath caught. Elam's rangy frame filled the room. The borrowed shirt and trousers fit as though they'd been made for him. Clad in the plain Amish garb, he looked like someone who had always belonged. Her brother's clothes were being used, and the world hadn't crumbled.

The oppressive weight of despair suddenly evaporated, replaced by a sensation of…relief? She'd believed survival meant leaving everything exactly as it was before that terrible day. But now she saw it differently. By honoring what had been, she could begin to focus on what might still be.

Bishop Graber checked his pocket watch. "Time's getting away. We should go."

"Sure thing," Elam agreed. "Ready when you are."

"See you tomorrow?" Nathan asked.

Elam flashed a grin. "Count on it." He gave a nod to the room. "I'll be back."

Bidding a final farewell, the two men headed outside.

Following them to the door, Anika watched as they prepared to depart. The ache hadn't vanished, but it had eased. Sorrow and loss still lingered, but they no longer weighed her down like a millstone. She'd been given a blessing, the chance to begin anew.

Without thinking, she dashed outside, calling after them. "Bishop, are volunteers still needed?"

James Graber paused, turning. "Why do you ask?"

"I want to help make the meals again," she blurted. "Like I used to."

The old man's eyes crinkled. "Are you sure that's something you could handle?"

"*Ja*," she insisted. "When can I?"

"How about tomorrow?"

Anika nodded. Tomorrow was a fresh start, and with it came a new purpose.

Surprise flickered across Elam's face. "You're really going to?"

"I am," she declared, and meant it.

She was prepared to take the first steps. Toward healing. Toward hope. Toward the future still waiting for her to claim it.

Today, she chose to live.

Chapter Eight

Another day dawned, bringing with it the steady rhythm of the Glick farm. Elam moved through the morning with more confidence, helping Reuben dress, feeding livestock alongside Nathan, and then tackling repairs. The hours passed quickly, the kind that wore on the body but quieted the mind. Now that he knew the routine, the bishop's assignment felt less burdensome, grounding him in a way he hadn't expected.

By late morning, it was time to shift gears. His community service hours at the center weren't optional.

Put in your time there and move on.

As they crossed toward the shed behind the barn, Nathan cast him a sideways glance. "You're really taking the buggy?"

"Looks like it," Elam said, leading the horse with an easy hand.

"That thing hasn't moved in ages," Nathan muttered. "Not since—well, you know. *Poppi* usually takes me in his if I need to go anywhere."

"It will today," he said, looping the mare's lead around a hitching post. "If Anika gets overwhelmed and needs to leave, she won't have to wait for someone to give her a ride. I talked to Reuben this morning about it, and he agrees."

"She *said* she'd go." Nathan frowned, skeptical. "Doesn't mean she will."

"Guess we'll find out," Elam said, grasping the handle of the shed's double doors. With a creak, both swung wide. Inside, the buggy sat like a relic, its black paint dulled under a layer of dust. The air smelled of tack leather, dry wood and old oil, familiar, comforting odors that tugged at half-buried memories.

Handing Mossie's reins to Nathan, he stepped inside and ran a hand along the buggy's weathered sideboard. Grime coated his fingers, but the wood beneath felt solid. He crouched to inspect the wheels, gave the axle a glance, then bounced the frame lightly. The springs creaked but held steady.

"It looks sound," he commented. "Could use a good cleaning, is all."

Nathan lingered near the door. "You want some help?"

"I've got it." Gripping the shafts, Elam rolled the buggy out into the sunlight. He popped open the side compartment and pulled out the harness, the worn leather smelling faintly of equine sweat and saddle soap. Draping the breast collar over one arm, he crossed to the mare and slipped the bridle over her ears, settling the bit in her mouth before fastening the cheek straps and throatlatch.

Nathan watched from a few feet away. "How long since you hitched one of these up?"

Elam gave a half shrug as he buckled the martingale. The mare flicked her ears but didn't fidget. "Five, maybe six years. Not since I learned to drive. After that, buggies were history."

"I'd like to learn to drive. A car, I mean."

"I can teach you," Elam offered, swinging the harness onto the mare's back and aligning the saddle pad. He cinched the girth with a pull, then adjusted the breeching before walking the shafts into place. The mare stirred with annoyance but stood as he guided them alongside her flanks. Checking the traces, he snapped them into the tug loops. Though it had been a while, the steps came back easily.

Nathan's eyes lit. "Really?"

"Sure. No reason you shouldn't know. It's a useful skill."

Kneeling, he checked each wheel bolt, giving them a firm twist, then stood and brushed the dust from his hands. "Can't do it now. But when I get my license back, I will."

"That would be neat," Nathan said, grinning.

Elam glanced over, surprised by how much the kid's excitement hit him. He hadn't known Nathan long, but he liked the teen. The boy was sharp, curious, always digging for answers. He'd never had a little brother, but if he did, Nathan would be the kind he'd want around.

Being the youngest of six, he'd learned early to make his own fun. His two eldest brothers were from his father's first marriage. After their mother passed, his father remarried and went on to have four more *youngies*. By the time he came along, his older siblings were already moving into their adult lives, leaving him on his own. Life had been steady until the wreck that claimed his parents. After that, the family splintered.

Not sure where he fit anymore, he'd drifted toward the outside world. He found he preferred *Englisch* ways—the freedom, the noise, the chance to make his own decisions—even if it came at a cost.

With a few final tugs to make sure the harness was snug and balanced, he stepped back. "Looks like this thing's ready to roll."

"Let's give it a try," Nathan said, stumping ahead on his crutches.

Gripping the reins, Elam clicked his tongue and guided the horse around the side of the barn and toward the front of the house. The old buggy's wheels creaked, but the roll was smooth enough. He kept the pace slow, letting the mare settle into an easy trot. They pulled up to the front gate and came to a stop. Beyond the fence, the porch sat quiet.

No sign of Anika.

Elam slipped his phone from his pocket and checked the time. They were cutting it close. "We're going to be late."

"Want me to go check?" Nathan offered.

"Stay with the buggy. I'll go. If she's not ready, I'll have to call someone else for a ride." With that, he pushed through the gate and headed up the walk, concern tightening in his chest.

She probably changed her mind. It could all be too much, too soon.

Inside, Reuben sat in the living room, a half-carved bird nestled in his lap. His sharp knife moved with care, and fine curls of wood drifted onto the newspaper spread on the floor beneath his wheelchair.

"Buggy's ready," he said, jerking a thumb over his shoulder. "Is she?"

Reuben glanced up. "She's a little nervous, but that's to be expected. I don't know what you did, but it's the first time she's let herself look forward to something."

Elam didn't answer right away. Reuben didn't know the guilt Anika carried, and he wasn't about to betray her trust. "I'm just trying to be a friend. That's all."

"Well, I'm glad," Reuben said, flicking a few wood shavings off his lap. "I was worried the two of you wouldn't mix. But *Gott*'s got a way of putting the right people in the right place, even when nobody else sees it coming."

"Yeah," he said, shoving his hands in his pockets. "I guess He does." Shifting nervously, he added, "Could you give Anika a little nudge? We're running late, and I don't want to keep Pastor Jensen waiting." It was only his second day, and he needed to show he was reliable about showing up.

"Of course." Reuben raised his voice, calling toward the hallway. "Anika?"

A pause followed, long enough for doubt to creep in. Then came the sound of footsteps, slow and hesitant. Down the hall, a bedroom door creaked open.

Anika stepped into view, not in her usual gray work dress, but in a soft blue frock that hugged her shoulders and swayed just above her ankles. A crisp white apron was tied neatly at her waist, and her *kapp* framed her face. A nervous flush colored her cheeks.

Seeing her, something tightened in Elam's stomach. That same strange feeling that always came when he looked at a pretty girl, only stronger now.

He looked at her, searching for the right words. "You look, um, nice," he said, his tongue suddenly heavy and clumsy for reasons he couldn't explain.

Anika glanced down, smoothing a wrinkle in her apron. "*Danke.* I wanted to look decent. It's been so long since I've been out."

"You do," Elam said, unable to look away. "Look decent."

The words landed flat, and he winced. *Decent? Really?* Of all the things he could've said, that was the best he could manage. It felt like his tongue had tied itself in knots.

They stood there, each looking at the other, the space between them charged with something unspoken. Neither moved. Just standing. Just looking.

Reuben cleared his throat. "Shouldn't you be getting on?"

Elam blinked, the brief enchantment breaking. "Yeah, you're right," he said, reaching for the backpack he'd left near the front door. This time, he'd come prepared. Returning Jason's clothes, he'd brought his own to change into after the morning chores were done. Slipping back into Amish garb felt like playing dress-up. Everything fit, but nothing felt right. "You ready?"

Anika hesitated. Her hands knotted together, gaze flicking with indecision. "I don't know if I can…"

"Bishop Graber said not to push if it frightens you."

She didn't answer, the silence stretching.

Reuben set aside the carving in his lap and rolled closer. "Do you remember the Bible study we had last night?" he asked gently. "The story of David and Goliath?"

Anika nodded. "*Ja.*"

"David was afraid, too," her father continued. "But he still stepped onto that battlefield. Not because he was fearless or strong, but because he trusted *Gott.*"

Her lips parted, maybe to argue. But no words came.

Reuben leaned forward. "Courage isn't about not being afraid," he said, reaching for her hand. "It's about moving forward despite the fear. Lean on Him, *mei dochder.* That's where your strength comes from."

Anika stood frozen, uncertainty flickering in her eyes. Then she drew a steady breath and lifted her chin. "I can do this."

A smile curved Reuben's lips. "The battle belongs to the Lord," he reminded. "And He's the one who goes before you."

"I won't let you down, *Dat.*" Leaning down, Anika pressed a quick kiss to her father's cheek. Squeezing his hand, she turned to Elam. "I'm ready."

Observing the exchange, Elam felt a surge of emotion. He couldn't explain why it stirred him so deeply, only that it did. The giants were different these days, but they still had to be faced.

"Your chariot awaits, milady," he said, pushing open the screen door.

Anika stepped onto the porch, pausing to wave back at her father before continuing down the steps.

Reuben rolled his wheelchair closer to the doorway so he could watch their departure. "Please, take care of her."

"I will," Elam promised. "She's in good hands."

Outside the front gate, the buggy stood waiting. Mossie pawed idly at the ground.

Approaching the buggy, Elam slid the side door open. "It's a bit dusty inside."

"Didn't have time to clean it up," Nathan added, wiping a hand across the surface.

Anika hesitated. Uncertainty flickered in her expression.

Elam noticed. "You don't have to go."

Anika didn't move. A long minute ticked away, followed by

another. Then, something visibly altered in her. Not a sudden change, but a quiet spark of resolve.

"I said I would, and I will." Without another word, she stepped forward, gripped the door frame, and climbed in. She settled on the hard bench, posture steady, eyes forward.

Nathan let out a low whistle. "Well, I'll be."

Anika leaned to look out, her voice calm. "Tell *Daed* I'll be just fine."

"I will," Nathan called back, grinning.

She looked to Elam. "Let's go."

"Yes, ma'am." Adjusting his cap, Elam climbed up and settled on the hard seat. The cab was small and plain, built for practicality rather than comfort. A narrow window at the front gave the driver a view of the road ahead. It smelled faintly of leather, dust and horses, an earthy scent that clung to every surface. Lifting the reins, he shot her a glance. "You sure?"

"I don't know." A little tremor moved her. "But if I don't try now, I might never try again."

Elam didn't blink. For a second, he just looked at her, really looked. The set of her jaw. The strength behind it. She was afraid, but she was going to town anyway.

That, he thought, *is true bravery.*

It struck him then how steadying it must be to lean on God. To face the unknown and still believe you're not alone.

Something cracked inside him, silent but aching. He didn't have that kind of conviction. Never had. Witnessing Anika carrying her burden by putting her trust in a higher power stirred a yearning he couldn't ignore. More than anything he wanted that strength, that unwavering light of grace. The desire was there, hovering just out of his reach.

Fingers tightening on the reins, he pressed his lips together. *Do I even deserve it?*

He didn't know.

But he wanted to believe he did.

* * *

Humble's Community Fellowship Hall stood like a quiet sentinel. The small white building with its peaked roof and hand-hewn cedar porch had served generations of townsfolk and farm families. It was solid, built by local Amish and *Englisch* hands, bound by a shared belief in neighborly work. A wooden sign above the door read, Fellowship in Action, its letters carved and painted by a long-ago carpenter. Marigolds blazed in the flower beds, and an American flag fluttered beside a wooden bench.

Anika tensed as Elam guided the buggy beneath the covered shelter. A lanky boy of about twelve with straw-colored hair and an eager stride dashed over.

"I'll take care of this for you," he called, reaching for the bridle.

Elam set the handbrake and opened the side door. "She's kept a steady pull, so she's warm."

"I'll get her watered and cooled down," the boy replied, tying the lead to the hitching rail. "And I'll clean up if she leaves anything."

Anika smiled, stepping down. "Haven't seen you in a while, Jimmy."

The boy's eyes lit up. "Didn't expect to see you. How've you been?"

"I'm doing better today," she said. "Just needed space after… everything."

"I get it," Jimmy said. "How's your *daed*? And Nathan?"

"They're managing." Most folks knew the story. Life didn't pause for grief; it pressed forward. The Bible said there was a season for everything: mourning, healing, moving on.

Jimmy nodded. "*Gut* to hear."

Elam adjusted his collar. "Ready to go in?"

Anika looked toward the open windows of the community center, where the clatter of pots and soft voices drifted out. "*Ja*. I am."

Elam offered a smile and fell into step beside her.

Anika paused in the doorway, heart tugging. She'd stood here countless times beside her *mamm*, humming gospel hymns while working. The memories surged, and for a heartbeat, she could hear *Mamm*'s voice, low and full of love. She blinked hard, but a tear slipped free.

"Something wrong?" Elam asked, concerned.

She swiped her cheek. "Just remembering all the times I was here before."

"If it's too much, you can go home."

"*Nein.*" Her voice steadied. "I'm going to do this."

One step at a time.

"Let's go inside." Elam pulled the door open. "Ladies first."

Walking inside, Anika was enveloped by voices and movement. It felt familiar yet foreign after so long.

"Anika! Well, now!" Ruthie Stoltzfus rushed over, pulling her into a firm hug. "It does my heart *gut* to see you, child. I've missed you."

Anika returned the embrace. "I missed you, too."

"Look who made it back!" Mary Lapp waved cheerily. "So happy to see you!"

Other faces turned her way with smiles and greetings.

Anika scanned the room, seeing familiar faces and a few new volunteers who waved. Everyone was friendly.

A lanky guy in cargo shorts and a faded hoodie strolled in, sunglasses perched on his nose. "Nice fez," he muttered, tugging at her *kapp*. "Does this come in other colors, or is white the only fashion option in prison?"

Anika jerked back. "Please don't."

The stranger smirked. "What? Can't take a joke?" He reached for her *kapp* again.

"Back off," Elam snapped, stepping forward. "That's enough."

The stranger grinned. "What? Free country." He spread his hands mockingly. "I've got every right to chat up this chick."

"She's with me," Elam said, closing the distance. "And you can keep your hands off."

"Relax, man." The guy snorted. "Just having fun."

"It's not fun," Elam said, voice icy. "It's disrespectful, and she doesn't like it."

The man smirked. "You going to make me behave?"

Elam didn't flinch. "Yeah, I am. There's no reason to make fun of people just because they're different."

"What's it to you?" the stranger snapped back.

"Because I'm Amish, too," Elam said. "And I'm no one you want to mess with."

The stranger stepped forward, squaring his shoulders. "You think you can take a piece of me?"

"I know I can."

Refusing to be intimidated, Anika laid a hand on Elam's arm. "Don't. He's not worth getting into trouble."

Relenting, Elam backed off. "You're right."

The guy sneered. "Real tough. Letting a little girl hold you back." He dragged a finger down his cheek in mock tears. "You people are pathetic."

Ruthie's voice rang out. "That's enough, Dylan!" Hands on hips, she pointed to the door. "You've done nothing but complain since you arrived. If you don't like it, there's the door."

Dylan's grin faltered as the room went still, eyes watching with discomfort. "I was just joking," he muttered, slouching toward the coffee station. "This place is boring and stupid." He threw himself into a chair.

Anika adjusted her *kapp*. "*Gott* still has some shaping to do with that one." Oddly, she hadn't felt afraid, only awe. Elam had stood up for her with calm strength. She felt protected.

"Who is that creep?" Elam asked, keeping a close eye.

Ruthie crossed her arms. "His name's Dylan Knox. And he's trouble with a capital T."

"What's he doing here?" Elam asked.

"Community service," Ruthie said, lowering her voice. "Public intoxication. Underage drinking. Couldn't pay the fine, so he got sent here to work it off. He's mad and wants everyone else to be miserable, too."

"No excuse to act like a jerk," Elam said, flexing his hands.

"He won't be here much longer," Ruthie promised. "I'll report him to his compliance officer."

Before the conversation could spiral into more gossip, one of the volunteers leading the program approached.

Pastor Mark Jensen, a tall man in crisp slacks and a black shirt with a white collar, offered a smile, but not his hand. "Anika, it's good to see you again. We've missed you."

Appreciating the courtesy, Anika dipped her head. "*Danke*, Pastor." Among the Amish, handshakes weren't common, especially between men and women. It wasn't that they were unfriendly. It was simply their way.

Jensen turned to Elam. "And you're late, young man. Planning to make a habit of it?"

Elam shook his head. "Sorry, Pastor. It won't happen again."

"You're here now, so let's get you to your places." He gestured toward the bustle. "Elam—plating and packing like yesterday. Anika, we need your skills in the kitchen. It's nearly noon."

"I'm on it." Elam gave a quick wave and hurried off.

Ruthie nudged Anika. "Come on, then," she said, giving an encouraging smile. "Time's getting away, and we've got a lot of catching up to do."

Nodding, Anika fell into step beside her. The kitchen was bright and bustling—massive cookstoves roared, wide counters gleamed, and shelves brimmed with staples. Everything was just as she remembered.

"You can do the cornbread," Ruthie said, pointing to the ingredients. "Mix fast. Hungry folks are waiting."

Anika's gaze settled on the counter. For a second, she could picture *Mamm* there, her laughter bubbling. The memory wrapped around her like a bittersweet embrace.

She wouldn't want me to be sad.

Pressing a hand to her middle, she drew a steadying breath. No panic. No freezing. Cornbread didn't need a recipe; it was something passed down through generations. A staple at nearly every meal, it was easy to make and satisfying. Focusing on the ingredients, she began to mix.

Throwing herself into the work, Anika moved from task to task—wiping counters, sweeping the floors, carrying out trash. For the first time, her mind quieted. Today, she wasn't alone. She was part of something bigger, something benefiting those in need. Despite differences in background and dress, everyone worked side by side. *Englisch* women in jeans, Amish women in dresses and coverings. Laughter flowed freely. The kitchen hummed with purpose.

By the time the delivery vehicles rolled out, they'd packed over two hundred meals. She glimpsed Elam a few times, but neither had more than a second to exchange a nod.

As she finished putting away the leftovers, Ruthie's hand brushed her shoulder.

"I'm glad you came," Ruthie said, giving a gentle squeeze. "I've been worried."

Anika's nerve momentarily faltered. Forcing herself to calm, she refused to let the old fears stir. "I just needed time."

"I understand," Ruthie agreed, nodding. "But I am surprised to see you showing up with Elam Mueller. After what he did to Nathan—"

A flicker stirred in Anika's chest. Memory of Elam standing up for her brought a warmth she hadn't expected.

"He's been forgiven."

"Then I can't fault him," Ruthie replied, her expression turning thoughtful. "Bishop Graber said he's prayed Elam would find his way back. Maybe this is a fresh start."

"I believe it is," Anika said.

For Elam. And for herself.

She realized then how much she'd come to rely on him. Not just for the practical help he offered, but for the way he seemed to understand her, to meet her halfway even when words failed. His patience felt endless, his presence steady in a way that made the world seem just a little less heavy. What she'd once viewed as an unwelcome burden now brought a quiet comfort that lingered long after he was gone.

A fluttering hope suddenly stirred in her chest, light and fragile, yet impossible to ignore. Could there ever be more between them than the steady comfort of his company?

Chapter Nine

Elam tugged the strap of his backpack tighter over his shoulder and stood outside, watching as the last few volunteers trickled out of the building. The noon shift had wrapped. Meals cooked and stacked in the delivery crates, the vans had rolled out for deliveries, and the Fellowship Hall was quiet again.

He pulled out his phone and checked his messages. Still nothing back from Jace. The last text mentioned that he was slammed at work and would get back to him. Then nothing more. And the three other guys he'd had texted either hadn't read the messages or were just too busy to reply.

He slipped the phone back into his pocket, jaw tight. He hated waiting around for a lift, and a rideshare was out of the question; with work dry and his savings running low, every dollar counted. Around the community center, people milled about, but he hesitated to approach anyone. Pride, and maybe a little embarrassment, kept him rooted in place.

Ask Anika?

Elam glanced across the lot. She was laughing with Sarah Miller and the Bontrager sisters, her face alight with a rare, unguarded smile. She didn't smile like that often. He couldn't bring himself to interrupt. Not when she looked so happy. Besides, it would mean putting her out of her way, and he wasn't about to be that guy.

Seeing her like this, surrounded by friends, gave him pause.

Everyone had welcomed her back without fuss. No pity. No awkward questions. She'd been gone a while, and now she was here. That was enough. No one needed to say why.

Taking one last look, he shrugged. *Guess I'll hoof it.*

Hitching his backpack higher, he turned toward the street and started down the sidewalk.

Settling into a steady rhythm, his sneakers shuffled against the sidewalk. A skateboard, or an e-bike, would help solve his problem. Anything that would help him get around and wouldn't depend on someone else's schedule.

Lost in his thoughts, he didn't hear the familiar rhythm of hoofbeats on asphalt until they were almost upon him.

"Hey," Anika called, pulling up beside him. "Where are you going?" The mane of her chestnut horse danced in the breeze as she guided it to a stop.

Elam halted. "Home."

Anika's brow furrowed. "Why didn't you wait for me?"

"You were visiting, and I didn't want to be a bother." He gestured vaguely. "Besides, I live clear across town. It's not the direction you'd be going anyway."

Anika rolled her eyes. "Don't be silly. I'll give you a ride, anywhere you need to go. Get in."

"You sure?"

"If I weren't, I wouldn't be here."

He shrugged. "If you say so."

"I do." She nodded. "Come on. It's too hot to be out."

Sliding open the buggy's door, Elam climbed in and set his backpack at his feet. "Thanks."

"You're welcome," she said, giving the leads a gentle flick. The buggy lurched forward, wheels creaking as the horse picked up a steady trot. Neither of them spoke at first. Only the rhythmic clop of hooves and the soft jingle of harness bells filled the silence between them.

Elam glanced over. "How's it feel, being out again?"

Anika's mouth twitched, as if she wasn't sure whether to laugh or cry. "Strange," she admitted. "Like I've been frozen inside, and now I'm starting to thaw."

He nodded, watching how the breeze teased a loose wisp of hair across her cheek. "Fear can be louder than reason sometimes. Makes it hard to hear anything else."

"I think I finally got tired of listening." Her voice wavered but didn't break. "I kept waiting for the ache to go away, for everything to feel normal again. But it doesn't. It won't. No matter how hard I pray, *Mamm* and Jason aren't coming back."

"Much as I hate to admit it, that's the hard truth. It's something we all face in our lives. People we love are going to pass away and we've got to deal with it."

She turned her head, just enough to give him a sideways glance. "I've figured out that it's time to stop chasing what was. This is my new normal."

"Time moves on, same as the seasons," Elam said, offering a small nod. "Doesn't mean we have to forget those we've lost. Just means we find a way to carry them with us, even as we go on living."

Anika blinked fast, then offered a tentative smile. "I'm trying." Giving her head a little shake, she glanced ahead at the upcoming stop sign. "You need to tell me where to go."

"Take a right," Elam said, pointing. "From here, we'll have to go through downtown to get to my place."

"Got it." The mare turned obediently, easily merging into the flow of vehicles.

Nearing the busier section of town, the afternoon traffic thickened. The streets and sidewalks were busy with people coming and going, focused on their errands. The hum of everyday life filled the air. Folks had places to go and things to do, part of the routine that kept the local merchants open. Many of the storefronts reflected a community woven from two worlds, each finding its place under the same sky.

"Turn there," he directed, pointing. "We'll pass the mercantile and the diner."

Anika did as instructed. "I haven't been to this side of town much," she murmured, looking every which way.

As they continued, Elam's gaze drifted to the corner where his favorite hangout stood. With its brick facade, green-and-gold-striped awning, and vintage painted lettering on the front window that read Millie's, the place had a timeless charm. Known for its oversized hamburgers and homemade pies, the café had been a downtown staple for generations, a place where everyone from farmers to city council members came to swap stories over coffee.

"Want to stop and get something?" he asked. "It's on me."

A spark lit her eyes. "I'd like that." She looked around. "Where do I park?"

"They have a place for buggies around back," he said.

Anika followed his direction, guiding the horse around to the shaded area behind the building. Local businesses offered accommodations for their Plain customers, offering dedicated buggy parking. Thoughtful touches like buckets of water left out for the horses made all the difference.

Walking around to the entrance, Elam held the door as they stepped inside. A favorite hangout, the eatery blended classic comfort with small-town nostalgia. The wooden floor creaked softly underfoot, and each booth featured a miniature jukebox, softly glowing and ready to play old tunes with the drop of a coin. A chalkboard behind the counter listed the daily specials. A counter was lined with stools and anchored an old-fashioned soda fountain with gleaming chrome taps and glass syrup bottles. A corner shelf held a stack of local newspapers, and the scent of brewed coffee hung in the air.

A waitress in a crisp white apron over a pale blue blouse and skirt greeted them. "Elam, long time no see."

"Hey, Lula," he called back. "You save my regular spot?"

"Kept it empty just for you, doll."

"Appreciate it." Giving her a wave, he led Anika to a booth by the window. The seat gave a familiar creak as he slid in. Being a bachelor, he didn't bother cooking much. His kitchen was barely more than a sink and a hot plate. "I hang out here a lot. The food's pretty good."

"I've never been here." Anika looked around, her wide eyes taking in everything. "*Mamm* always said it was a waste of money to eat out when you have food at home."

Elam didn't get the chance to respond before Lula arrived with a tray of ice water and two laminated menus.

"What can I get you?"

Anika offered a polite smile. "Just a *kaffee*, please."

Elam shook his head. He remembered what Reuben had said, how his daughter had never really gotten a proper *rumspringa*. That didn't sit right with him. Not today. She deserved a treat.

"Belay that," he said, handing the menus back. "We'll take two deluxe banana splits." He wasn't thinking when he'd invited Anika out. It had just...happened. Somehow, he'd work it into his budget. Beans and rice were filling enough, and she didn't need to know how thin his wallet was. She deserved a little fun, and he was determined she'd have it.

Lula grinned. "With extra whipped cream and nuts?"

"The works," Elam said, winking.

"Coming right up."

"Dessert? In the middle of the day?" Anika asked.

Elam leaned back, one arm draped along the booth. "We did a good day's work. Why not celebrate?"

A spark lit her eyes. "Oh, let's do. I haven't had any fun in the longest time."

"Then let's go all out." Fishing out some change, he nodded toward the jukebox on the wall. "Pick something."

She took a quarter, her eyes scanning the rows of titles, country classics from the '50s through the '80s. Then, with a mischievous grin, she pushed the coin into the slot and jabbed a button. A twangy trumpet intro burst from the speakers, unmistakable in its fiery rhythm.

Elam raised a brow. "Wasn't expecting a pick from the Man in Black."

"You think I'm all stuffy and boring?"

He chuckled. "A little."

She grinned. "Well, you're wrong."

The waitress returned with their banana splits, vanilla ice cream dripping with chocolate, pineapple and strawberry sauce, and crowned with whipped cream and chopped pecans.

"This is huge," Anika said, scooping up a bite. "Don't know if I can finish it."

"Millie's makes the best," Elam replied, digging into his own.

Time slipped away after that. The jukebox played on, each taking turns with the selections: slow songs full of longing, upbeat ones that made them laugh. Conversation flowed easily, drifting from music to favorite foods, from childhood stories to silly mishaps they hadn't shared with anyone else.

Outside, the world moved on without them.

The day had unfolded nothing like Elam had planned. It had turned out better. Watching Anika laugh, seeing the way her eyes lit up with each song and story, something settled in his chest. Deep and certain, it was impossible to ignore.

He liked being with her.

More than he probably should.

Anika slowed as they turned onto a narrow street lined with weathered brick buildings and fading signs. Some still bore the names of old businesses, but most were boarded up or converted into homes.

She pulled up in front of a squat cinder-block structure with peeling paint and a faded sign hanging over a wide bay door. An old beater of a work truck was parked nearby.

"This is it," Elam said, opening the buggy's side door. "Home sweet garage."

Anika blinked, surprised. "You live here?"

He nodded. "There's a loft upstairs. Small apartment, not much to see. Mostly I'm downstairs in the shop."

She looked up at the few small windows near the roofline. The idea sounded strange, but somehow it seemed fitting for him.

He glanced back at her, hopeful. "Want to come inside?"

Anika hesitated. A girl alone with a man in his home, unchaperoned, wasn't allowed. "I don't think it would be proper."

He laughed, not unkindly. "We'll just be in the shop. The bay door will stay open. Anybody driving by can see us, plain as day. And trust me, my living space isn't a showplace."

Her cheeks warmed at his teasing. "All right, then. Just for a minute." Though she needed to get home and put supper on the table, she wasn't ready for the day to end. The afternoon had slipped by too quickly. She'd enjoyed every minute with Elam. He was funny in a way that caught her off guard, and she found his dark eyes and amiable smile hard to ignore.

If only he were Amish, she thought, *he'd be the perfect boyfriend.*

"Come on. I'll show you around."

Elam slipped a key into the padlock and heaved the heavy bay door open, the metal groaning in protest. With a flick of a switch, the overhead lights buzzed to life, casting a stark phosphorescent glow over the space.

"This is it," he invited, stepping inside.

Anika followed, looking every which way. Tools hung in tidy rows along the walls, each one placed with care. In the corner, a scuffed leather recliner sat beside a dorm fridge doubling as a side table, an old radio atop. The air smelled oily, a strange but not unpleasant scent that reminded her of farm equipment and tools.

"It's different."

Shoving his hands in his pockets, Elam glanced around. "Yeah. It's just temporary." He met her gaze, his voice steady. "I've got plans for a real home, someday." He shrugged, offering a lopsided smile. "Losing my job set me back, but that won't last forever." An embarrassed shrug rolled off his shoulders. "At least, I hope not."

Her gaze drifted toward the back of the bay, where a large shape sat beneath a snug gray cover. "What's that?"

Face breaking into a grin, Elam walked over. "Hang on. I'll show you." He pulled the cover off, revealing a sleek, low-slung car painted deep metallic blue. Chrome trim caught the overhead lights. "My pride and joy."

"It's pretty," Anika said, stepping closer. "What is it?"

His grin spread. "That's a 1970 Dodge Challenger R/T."

Meaning nothing, it all went over her head. "Which is?"

"It's a classic," he explained. "From back when companies were all about speed and power. This one has a four-twenty-six Hemi engine. That's top-of-the-line. Real rare." Running a hand over the vehicle's smooth hood, he grinned. "It was going to be crushed for scrap when I rescued it."

"And you fixed it up?"

"Completely," he said, satisfaction lacing his voice. "Took me three years. Hunted down the parts, rebuilt the engine and rewired the whole system. A couple of friends helped me with the bodywork and paint."

Anika stepped closer, her gaze sweeping over the car's gleaming finish, the careful detailing. It was hard to believe it had once been junkyard wreckage. She'd known he was good with his hands, but this was more than skill. He'd taken a pile of rusted parts and rebuilt them into something remarkable.

"What do you do with something like this?"

A faint smile tugged. "Right now? Nothing much." His expression turned rueful. "Lost my license, remember? I've only gotten to take it out once or twice, just around the block." His gaze drifted over the vehicle's sleek curves, lingering with silent longing. "One day, I'll get to race it."

Race.

The word immediately sent an icy shiver down Anika's spine. "I wish you wouldn't."

Elam looked away, then his hand settled firmly on the hood. "I know it's dangerous." His voice was low. "But I can't part with it. Not yet." He glanced back at her, a hopeful spark lighting his eyes. "Want to sit inside?"

The idea of being so close to something so powerful gave her pause. But seeing the quiet pride in his eyes, she nodded. "Okay. Just for a minute."

Elam hurried around, opening the passenger-side door. "Your ride awaits, milady."

Dipping her head, Anika slid into the seat. Inside, the car felt different from anything she'd known, wide seats that felt firm beneath her, a big steering wheel on the driver's side and a dashboard filled with round dials glinting faintly in the dim light. She didn't understand their purpose, but they made the car feel alive. The interior smelled faintly of leather and new carpeting.

Elam got in behind the wheel. "Feels different from the inside, doesn't it?" He reached for the ignition, cranking the key. The engine roared to life, a low, steady purr vibrating with pure power. To him, the vehicle was more than metal and wheels. It was a dream waiting to roar to life.

Anika froze. The speed, the power, the reckless freedom this machine promised made her skin crawl. It felt like a trap, a dark shadow lurking just beneath the excitement, whispering danger she couldn't shake. Her pulse hammered as panic tightened its grip, squeezing breath and reason alike. She fought to steady herself, but the walls of the car seemed to close in, the interior too confining. The pulsing glow of the dashboard lights flickered like watchful eyes.

With a sharp inhale, she climbed out. "I should go home."

He shut off the engine and followed. "You all right?"

Anika swallowed, trying to tamp down the unease clawing at her. "It's getting l-late," she stammered. "*Daed* and Nathan will be expecting me for supper."

"Okay. Let me walk you out."

She gave a nod, and together they stepped into the fading light of afternoon.

At the edge of the drive, he hesitated. "Are you going to be all right? Heading home alone, I mean?"

Anika drew a steadying breath and lifted her chin. Fear fluttered in her chest, but she refused to let it win. She could be nervous and still stand her ground. *Gott* would fight the hard battles for her.

"*Ja*," she said, managing a smile. "Of course."

He studied her. "You sure everything's okay?"

"Fine," she replied, too quickly, too lightly. "Just a little tired, that's all."

"It's been a long day," he agreed. "Go home. Get some rest."

"I will." She paused, then added softly, "*Danke* for today. It was…nice." On impulse, she rose to her tiptoes and brushed a kiss against his cheek. She didn't think. She just did. Elam didn't know it, but he'd become someone special. Someone who mattered.

Smiling, he touched the spot. "You're welcome."

Before her emotions could betray her, Anika hurried to the buggy and climbed inside. She'd been handling the reins since she was knee-high to a grasshopper, and her hands moved with practiced ease as she released the handbrake and guided the rig around the narrow drive. Sensing her urgency, Mossie broke into a brisk trot.

Trees and fences blurred past, but she barely noticed. Her

thoughts were already miles ahead. The steady rhythm of hooves on pavement should've calmed her, but it didn't. As much as she'd enjoyed spending time with Elam, the excitement of the day had drained away after he'd shown her the car, leaving behind a heaviness she couldn't shake.

Sleek. Beautiful. Dangerous.

Somewhere deep down, she knew Elam's fancy automobile wasn't just a machine.

It was trouble.

Chapter Ten

A week slipped away, then another, before Elam noticed time passing. Helping at the Glick farm and preparing meals for senior services, the days folded into each other, marked by the quiet rhythm of work. The sentence he'd dreaded had become a welcome routine.

Restless, he glanced around the empty community center. Saturday's deliveries were done, and the rest of the weekend stretched ahead. Before the accident, his social life meant loud music and louder friends. Losing his license had stripped away his freedom, adrenaline fix and fun. Now, most of his *Englisch* friends didn't call or text. Trouble had a way of clearing a room, and the message couldn't be clearer. He'd been cut loose. Loneliness cut deeper than he cared to admit.

Now what?

Pastor Jensen approached. "Hey there," he greeted. "Thanks for the work you've been doing."

Elam nodded. "You're welcome."

"Got a minute?"

"Sure."

The pastor didn't waste time. "Your community service wraps up next week."

Elam tensed, chest tightening. The pastor's signature was needed to verify his hours for the court. "That's right."

"Some folks stick around after their time's up," Jensen said. "I hoped you might be one."

"You want me to keep volunteering?"

"Absolutely." Jensen smiled. "Your skills are valuable. When the delivery van broke down, your fix was a lifesaver."

Elam shrugged, ducking his head. "Vacuum line to the intake manifold was cracked. The engine was stalling out every time it idled. Spliced in a new section and sealed it up. Wasn't a big deal."

"Maybe for you," Jensen said. "To us, it was a disaster."

"It's what I do," he joked. "Fix disasters, that is."

"Not everyone can," the pastor pointed out. "Ever thought about offering that as a service? Folks around here would welcome a mobile mechanic."

"You mean like make house calls?"

"Exactly."

"I've been thinking about starting my own business," he agreed, latching on to the suggestion. "I like driving a tow truck, but I want to be my own boss, set my own hours. That was the plan before everything went off the rails."

"It won't last forever," Jensen said. "Keep it in mind."

"I will," Elam replied. "Thanks for the idea. Anything to keep us wayward souls on the straight and narrow, right?"

Jensen's smile softened. "I've worked with truly lost folks, Elam. You're not one of them."

"I'd like to think I'm not all bad."

"You're not," the pastor said. "You're a young man who made a bad decision. Maybe it's because you're restless. Or you haven't found your purpose yet."

That struck deeper than Elam expected. "I thought I had it figured out. Now, I'm not sure."

"Oh? How so?"

"It's hard to explain." He hesitated. "Lately, I feel empty."

Jensen nodded. “That’s not uncommon. You might be missing a personal relationship with God.”

Elam’s chest tightened. “Sometimes I think that’s it. Other times, I don’t know.”

“My door’s always open,” Jensen said. “I know you were raised Amish, but if you can’t talk to Bishop Graber, I’m here. And we have nondenominational services every Sunday and Wednesday evenings if you’d care to attend. God’s door is always open.”

The conversation pressed heavily. Amish, yet not entirely, he stood on the fringes, uncommitted to his heritage, adrift. Joining another church would feel like he was betraying his birthright.

“I appreciate that,” he said, acknowledging the invitation without committing. “I’m not sure what comes after community service. I’d like to keep helping, but I can’t promise anything.”

“I understand.” Pausing in the doorway, Jensen asked, “See you Monday?”

“Definitely. Thanks, Pastor.”

“You’re welcome. Enjoy your weekend.” With a wave, Jensen left.

Elam stared at the closing door, the pastor’s words stirring a restless ache. He breathed deeply, wrestling with the uncertain path ahead.

Anika’s voice broke his thoughts. “Are you ready?”

Glancing up, Elam shook his head. Most days, Anika gave him a lift home before heading back to the farm, a trip that added extra miles to her day. No point in putting her out, especially when he didn’t care to be at the garage anymore. The place didn’t feel like home, just four walls and too much silence.

“I don’t think I’ll need a lift today.” He looked outside at the warm, bright afternoon. “I’ll walk.”

Surprise flickered across her face. “Your place is clear across town.”

"I know. Just don't want to be there right now."

Anika's gaze softened. "I feel that way sometimes," she admitted. "Even when I was too scared to leave the house, I felt trapped. Now, getting out, whenever I go home, it feels like the walls are closing in. I love Nathan and *Daed*, but caring for them…" She made a gesture of frustration. "It's the same every day."

"I get it," Elam said. She was trying to live normally, but she still held herself tightly, the distance between fear and routine fragile.

"I know I'm supposed to be grateful for a home and people who love me," she continued. "But sometimes, it feels like a burden."

"Then let's change things up a bit," he said, giving her a friendly nudge. "It's a nice day. Why don't we take a little time for ourselves?"

Her face lit up. "I'd like that."

They stepped out of the community center, down the paved walkway. A few stragglers waved goodbyes.

Side by side, they walked toward the covered horse shelter. When they reached the buggy, Anika ran her hand along the wooden edge of the door, then hoisted herself up.

"Where are we going?" she asked as Elam climbed up beside her and took the reins.

"Well…" He hesitated. "It's probably not all that exciting to a girl."

She smiled. "Try me."

"I'd like to check out some used car lots. Bishop Graber asked me to keep an eye out for a church van, but I haven't had the time yet."

"*Daed*'s been waiting for word, but he didn't want to nag you about it." Smoothing the folds of her dress across her knees, Anika glanced over with a smile. "I'd love to go look."

"Seriously?" Most girls didn't care about things like that. Cars and all.

She laughed. "Absolutely."

Elam held her gaze for a moment, then looked away before she could read too much. A shiver ran through him; part nerves, part something deeper he wasn't ready to name.

No, she wasn't like other girls. There was something about Anika that drew him in. Something he shouldn't let himself feel.

Suddenly aware of how close she sat, he shifted, creating distance. "We should get going." Releasing the handbrake, he gave the reins a gentle tug. With a soft creak, the buggy rolled forward. Mossie's hooves clopped steadily as they headed down the street.

Elam attempted to focus on the task ahead, but his thoughts kept straying. Anika's laugh echoed in his mind, the way she brushed her hair back, the steady confidence in her movements, the warmth of her presence… It all pulled at him when he least expected it.

He shook his head, hoping to clear the fog, and concentrated on Mossie and the road. But every glance at her reignited the warmth in his chest. He didn't understand it, didn't want to, and yet it refused to be ignored. Something about Anika Glick left him off balance, teetering on the edge of a feeling he wasn't ready to name.

The scents of supper filled the kitchen as Anika set the last dish on the table: fried chicken, mashed potatoes, green beans, with apple pie and home-churned vanilla ice cream for dessert.

"You've outdone yourself," *Daed* said, looking over the feast. "Why the extra effort?"

"A little celebration," she said, pulling out a chair.

Nathan's eyes sparked. "What's the occasion?"

Anika cast a quick look at Elam. He'd spent hours searching for a vehicle, and she couldn't let him go home to his empty garage. Inviting him for the evening meal felt right. His grateful smile said more than words. The gathering was the perfect way to end the week.

"Do you want to tell them, or can I?"

Elam looked mildly panicked. "Nothing's finalized yet."

Daed leaned forward. "I hope it's *gut* news."

Unable to wait another second, Anika burst out, "Elam's found a van for the church!"

Daed's eyes lit up. "Oh, my! That is wonderful."

"That's why we were gone all afternoon," Elam explained.

Anika nodded, adding, "Oh, *Daadi*, it's perfect."

"I can't disagree," Elam said, elbows on the table. "Newer model, well cared for, decent mileage."

"It'll do the job?" *Daed* asked.

"Without a doubt. Already partially modified, so less work."

Nathan straightened with interest. "Modified how?"

Anika jumped in. "It has a ramp and a lowered floor for easy access." She paused, glancing at Elam. "Did I get that right?"

He laughed. "Yeah, it's a good setup."

"And it runs?" Nathan asked.

"Needs a tune-up, a few other minor fixes," Elam explained. "Doesn't seem to be anything urgent. Just annoying."

"Sounds like it might be the one," Nathan said, grinning.

"Could be," Elam emphasized.

Anika stilled. "I thought you said it was the one."

"Oh, I believe it is," Elam said. "But the price is a stumbling point. The dealer's asking more than Bishop Graber's budget. The church doesn't have a lot to spend."

"How much over?" *Daed* asked.

"A couple thousand," Elam said with a sigh.

Daed's smile faltered. "That's not what I was hoping to hear."

"Don't let it weigh on you," Elam countered, raising a hand in reassurance. "Nothing's final yet. I'll take the bishop to see it soon as I can. Maybe we can talk the dealer down, especially once he understands it's for the church."

The conversation moved back and forth, shifting between cautious optimism and the sting of too many setbacks.

Anika's thoughts drifted to the long hours they'd spent walking through one car lot after the other. Time and again, they'd passed over vehicles that weren't mechanically sound or cost too much. This one had been different. Elam's eyes had lit up when he spotted it: clean lines, a strong engine, plenty of room inside. He'd inspected it from bumper to back seat like it already belonged to them.

"This doesn't mean it's out of reach," she said. "We've come this far. If it's meant to serve the community, *Gott* will make a way."

Daed's hands tightened. "I hate burdening others. Asking the bishop to spend more isn't right."

"There are other vans to be looked at," Elam said, choosing to be optimistic. "With patience, the right one will come."

"Why can't we refashion the buggy?" Nathan asked.

"I've thought about that," *Daed* said. "If I could roll in and out, I could handle the reins."

Elam sipped from his glass, setting it down. "It's not simple. A buggy's frame can't hold a wheelchair ramp's weight without reinforcing the rear and sides. The ramp's angle would be steep unless it's long or hinged, adding weight and storage issues. And widening the frame could throw off balance. With a wheelchair, a person and reinforcements, a single horse might not pull it safely."

"So, it'd need to be built from scratch?" *Daed* asked.

"Pretty much," Elam said. "Materials alone could cost eight to twelve thousand, even with volunteer labor."

Anika winced. "It sounds hopeless."

"The salesman's price and what he'll accept may differ," Elam said. "We'll get down to business after the bishop sees it.

If the guy says no, there are other vans. This one's a top contender, though. I could work with it."

"The easiest solution would be me walking again," *Daed* said, frowning. "As it is, I'm useless."

"That's not true," Anika said. "The doctors said there's a chance with therapy."

"I can't roll to appointments," *Daed* said. "Renting a van and driver, plus therapy, costs money. I'm not one for charity."

"What kind of therapy?" Elam asked.

"Building upper body strength, working my legs," *Daed* replied.

"He hasn't gotten a lick of treatment," Nathan said, eyeing his father. "He won't go because we can't pay much."

Frustration flickered in *Daed*'s gaze. "I'll accept help when I truly need it," he said, hands resting on the wheelchair arms. "But I can't keep taking it—not in good conscience. The Lord strengthens me in my weakness; I'll let His grace carry me, not endless charity from others."

"Pride won't fix your legs," Nathan countered.

Daed's jaw tightened. "I don't need a lecture, *sohn*. I know my limits, and I'll handle them my way."

Anika exhaled in frustration as the two went back and forth. How stubborn her father could be—always insisting on following his own path, no matter how hard the road was for those who loved him.

"We trust that you know what's best," she said, stepping in before the tension could flare further. Nathan sometimes needed reminding that backing off was an act of care, not defeat.

"I used to strength train with buddies," Elam mused. "Why not set up a gym here?"

Nathan stretched his leg, now cast-free. "I'm supposed to exercise. Maybe we could all work out together."

"That might be a *gut* idea," *Daed* said cautiously. "I can go at my own pace."

"Then that's what we'll do," Elam said.

The men discussed plans, their voices animated.

Anika listened, the casual suggestion shaping into something meaningful, bringing structure to their lives. Elam's calm confidence surprised her. He offered solutions, not excuses. His steady presence made her believe things would be all right.

Sensing her gaze, Elam turned. "What?"

"The food's getting cold," she said, reaching for the platter. "We should eat."

After a prayer, the food was passed, silverware clinking amid soft conversation, a simple fellowship.

Later, the sun dipped low, casting shadows across the porch. A cool breeze rustled as Anika walked Elam outside to say goodnight. He stood by the steps, hands in pockets, watching the driveway.

"You didn't have to call a ride," she said. "I could've taken you."

He shrugged. "Jace offered. Didn't want to make you drive back to town again."

"I don't mind. Gives me a reason to get out." She paused. "I didn't think I'd ever do that again. But I did. Because of you."

"I didn't do anything special."

"You did," she insisted. "You kept coming around when you weren't welcome. I couldn't have done that. You've been *gut* with *Daed* and Nathan. They like you."

His brows lifted. "They do?"

"*Ja.*"

His grin warmed. "That means a lot."

Silence lingered, gentle but charged.

Elam nudged the step with his boot. "Don't think I'm taking advantage, but maybe we could, you know, keep seeing each other."

Anika stilled. "Are you asking to walk about?"

"Yeah, I guess I am." His smile wavered. "Unless you'd rather I didn't."

Her pulse quickened. "It's not that I don't want to…"

"But?"

"I just don't know what to do with that. With us."

"It doesn't have to mean anything," he said, not pressing. "Just spend time together. You know, as friends."

The word hung heavily. Friends. She wasn't sure that's all she wanted, but it was where they needed to start.

"I'm going to church tomorrow. Want to come?"

He blinked. "Me?"

"Why not?"

"I haven't been in years." He looked away, jaw tightening. "What if I don't fit in?"

"You don't have to do anything," she said. "Just be there."

Elam was quiet, then his expression steadied. "All right," he agreed. "I'll go."

Anika's chest warmed at his words, a little spark of hope flaring inside her. She'd feared he'd push back, make excuses, or shrug her invitation off. Yet here he was, agreeing. Not because she demanded it, but because he trusted her enough to step into something unfamiliar.

It wasn't much, but it was enough to make her heart lift.

Chapter Eleven

Standing on the Mishler family's wide veranda, Elam adjusted the collar of his white shirt and ran a hand down the front of his dark blazer. His slacks were freshly pressed, the outfit chosen with care. His old Amish Sunday clothes still hung in the back of his closet, but he couldn't bring himself to wear them. It would've felt dishonest, even disrespectful, since he no longer belonged to the church. Still, he wanted to honor the moment. At least for today.

"Well, I'll be," Jacob Mishler said, his voice tinged with genuine surprise. "Elam Mueller—long time, no see."

Relief loosened the knot in Elam's chest. "*Danke* for having me," he said, shifting from one foot to the other. "I hope I'm not intruding. I can go if you'd rather not have someone like me here."

"Not at all." Giving him a look of approval, Jacob grinned. "Everyone who wants to hear the Lord's word is welcome in this *haus*."

"I appreciate that." Years had slipped by since he'd last seen Jacob, years marked by choices that had pulled them apart. Their lives had diverged, yet here he was, stepping back into a past he hadn't expected to return to.

"I'd heard you were under the bishop's watch," Jacob continued. "Wondered how that was going."

Elam's stomach tightened. The incident and everything that came after had made the local paper. He didn't need to guess whether people were talking. In a small town, gossip traveled fast, and the Plain community was no exception.

"It's going. I made a mistake, but I'm trying to fix it."

Jacob studied him, not with judgment, but with something quieter. "It's not a mistake if it's brought you back to church."

"Bishop Graber said I might try coming," Elam explained, glancing toward his companion. "And I was invited."

Anika stood beside him, a quiet presence in the soft morning light. She wore a simple black dress that fell modestly around her calves, paired with sensible boots. Long hair gathered into a bun at the nape of her neck, a few loose tendrils softened her profile. A crisp white prayer *kapp* framed her face, and the faintest flush from the early ride colored her cheeks, adding a glow to her complexion. Over one arm, she carried a wicker basket. Nestled inside was a spice cake, fragrant with hints of cinnamon and cloves.

Jacob's gaze lit up. "*Ach*, this is another joyous surprise."

Anika nodded. "It's *gut* to see you, Jacob."

"You've been away a long time," Jacob said. "I trust you are better?"

"*Ja*. I am."

"How's your *daed*? And Nathan?"

"They're doing well," she replied. "*Daed*'s having better days, and Nathan just got his cast off. He would have come, but he wanted to stay home and have Bible study with *Daed*."

"So Reuben's still not able to travel?" Jacob asked.

"*Nein*. Not yet. But *Mammi* and *Poppi* are visiting with him today, keeping him company. He always misses being here. Church has always meant a lot to him."

"I know how much Reuben loves the fellowship," Jacob said. "I hope he's able to get out more soon."

"We're getting closer," Anika said, her gaze lighting with hope. "Elam found a used van, one with a wheelchair ramp already installed. If all goes well, it'll make it easier for *Daed* to come to church again."

Jacob nodded, visibly moved. "I was one of the ones who voted in favor of updating the *Ordnung* for this. It wasn't an easy decision for some of the older folks, but it felt right. People like Reuben shouldn't be cut off from getting around because they can't ride in a buggy anymore."

"*Danke*, Jacob," Anika said. "It means a lot that the community has supported the need."

Jacob offered a kind smile. "We do what we can for each other. That's how it's always been." Looking at Elam, his expression grew thoughtful. "You may not see it now, but I believe *Gott*'s hand was in this. Even in the hard things, prayers have been answered in ways we couldn't have planned."

"I'm still figuring things out," Elam said. "But I'm willing to believe that maybe there's something bigger at work behind the scenes."

Jacob chuckled. "That's a *gut* way to see it. Sometimes faith grows best in the unknown." Stepping back, he indicated the small gathering waiting in the parlor. "Please, join us. We're still waiting on the minister, so we haven't started yet."

Elam relaxed. That was the way of most Plain folks. Slow to judge, quicker to forgive. No long-winded lectures, no dragging up the past. Though a few curious glances lingered on him longer than felt comfortable, most offered quiet acceptance, their nods and murmured greetings carrying acceptance. If anyone had an objection to his presence, they kept it to themselves.

Jacob gestured toward his *fraa*, who was seated nearby, cradling their newborn. "Naomi, my wife," he said proudly. "And my daughter, Miriam."

Naomi returned the smile. "Welcome," she murmured, smoothing the blanket covering the tiny *boppli.*

Seeing the pair, Anika's eyes lit up. "*Ach*, Naomi," she exclaimed, rushing to her friend's side. "You had the *kind*."

Despite the fatigue of new motherhood, Naomi beamed. "Six weeks to the day." The baby stirred, and she rocked a little more, her touch tender and practiced.

Anika leaned closer. "Look at all that dark hair. Just like Jacob's."

Naomi chuckled. "*Ja*, and the temper to match, if her cries mean anything." Her eyes sparkled. "She has a fine set of lungs."

The girls laughed, teasing each other as well as sharing the quiet camaraderie that came from caring for their families. Such was second nature to them. Amish women were raised to focus on the well-being of their homes and *youngies*, their lives marked by quiet devotion to the daily tasks that held their world together.

Amused, Elam watched. He couldn't remember the last time he'd been part of a scene so unguarded and full of simple joy. All his brothers and his sisters were married now, with houses full of little ones. Nieces and nephews he barely knew.

The realization left a hollow ache in his chest, a reminder of how far he'd let the divide between himself and his family grow. Why had he done it? Late nights, fast cars and video games. Shallow friendships with people who meant…nothing.

His throat tightened. How could he fix it? Around him, soft laughter and murmured greetings filled the room, sounds of belonging he'd once taken for granted.

"Any chance that's in your future?" Jacob asked, giving him that knowing elbow men used when they were ribbing a friend.

Elam forced a smile and shook his head. "Not in the cards for me. Not now, anyway."

"No one special?"

"Nah." Elam shrugged. "Not lately."

Even as he said it, his gaze drifted back to Anika. Kneeling beside her friend's chair, her eyes crinkled at the corners in a way he was starting to notice more than he should. Her lips were parted in a smile that tugged something deep in his chest. She looked so at home in this world of lullabies, of whispered prayers and Sunday quiet.

He imagined what it might be like to come home to a wife like her. To share quiet meals, to hear the patter of little feet on wooden floors, to know he was needed and loved.

The notion caught him off guard. It wasn't just the warmth of the parlor or the gathering itself, but a deeper ache. The longing to belong to something bigger than himself.

Another knock echoed through the house.

Jacob hurried to the door, opening it wide. A tall, broad-shouldered man stepped inside. Dressed in black, his beard was long and neatly trimmed. With him was a petite blonde woman with kind eyes, her arms gently guiding two identical little girls, their golden braids bouncing as they peered around curiously.

Elam froze. Oh, no. Not today.

Abram.

His older brother, a minister, was the model of righteousness—and the last person he'd expected.

"Sorry we're late," Abram apologized. "Got held up with the *kinder*."

"I figured you'd get here sooner or later," Jacob said, ushering them inside.

In the Humble community, the gatherings among neighbors in an allotted district were simple but deeply meaningful. Usually, half a dozen families from the same area came together to listen to sermons delivered by a minister appointed under the bishop's guidance. Services often stretched for several hours and were followed by a meal. It was less about ceremony and more about connection, the strengthening of faith, and the offering of support in both joy and hardship. All ministers rotated through the smaller, rural gatherings, each taking a turn to travel.

Hoping not to be noticed, Elam tried to blend in. It didn't work. His brother caught sight of him.

"If you'll excuse me, Jacob," Abram said. "There's someone I need to talk to."

Without waiting for a reply, he stepped away from his *fraa* and made a beeline for Elam. When Abram reached him, he didn't raise his voice. He didn't have to. The concern brewing in his gaze said enough.

"Brother," he said, placing a firm hand on his arm. "Outside. Now."

Acutely aware everyone was watching, Elam hesitated. The last time he'd spoken to Abram had been years ago, and the silence since then had become a chasm. Though they both lived in the same town, Humble was just big enough for them to avoid one another, moving in different circles and living very different lives.

But now, standing at the edge of the fold, he knew the reckoning between them could not be avoided.

"All right," Elam agreed, and followed his brother outside.

On the porch, the door closed behind them, Abram turned, arms folded. "What are you doing?"

"I came to hear the service."

Abram's brow furrowed. "After what you've been involved in, you think showing up to worship makes everything right?"

"I know what people are saying, and most of it is true. But I'm not here to mock the Lord. I came because I wanted to."

"Piousness isn't something to play at," Abram warned. "You've done a lot of harm. To the community, to our family, to others… That doesn't just go away with one Sunday in the pews."

Elam spread his hands. "I know. But I've started to rethink things."

"Is that right?"

"Yes."

"Why?" Abram asked.

"Before I got arrested, I did what I wanted, when I wanted, and didn't answer to anyone," Elam said. "Now that I've had to answer to the law and Bishop Graber, I've gotten a look at things from a different point of view."

"And what do you see?"

"I've realized what I left behind wasn't so terrible. So, when Anika invited me to church, I thought I'd come."

The tension in Abram's stance eased. "The bishop has kept me updated. Says you've been helping the Glick family. Doing fine work at the community center, too."

"That's right. I've made amends."

"At first, I was inclined to believe you had him fooled," Abram admitted, studying him closely. "But now… I'm not so sure."

"I'm trying to be better," Elam said. "I can't explain it exactly, but something's changing in me."

"Truly?" his brother asked, skeptical.

He nodded. "Yeah. And it's scaring me. But for the first time, I want more. Something real."

Abram studied him, then placed a hand on his shoulder. "A meaningful life starts with *Gott*. If you're willing to turn your life over to the Lord, He'll give you everything you're looking for. Not all at once, and not without struggle, but in His time, He'll make your life whole again."

Elam swallowed, a sharp twist of emotion knotting deep in his gut. Missing pieces were beginning to snap into place. "I think that's what I'm searching for."

Not just a path forward, but a way home.

The afternoon sun spilled through the parlor windows, painting golden streaks across the polished wooden floor and catching the edges of the women's white prayer coverings and the men's dark suits. As the final amen faded, a hush settled over the room, deep, sacred and still.

Cradling a worn copy of the *Ausbund*, Anika stood with the congregation. Following the minister's instruction, she opened the book to a familiar page printed in the old language. After a brief pause, the opening line of the hymn rose gently into the air, unaccompanied, slow and solemn.

Her voice joined the others. The German words flowed, rich

notes stretched long and low, swelling with depth and meaning. The melody, simple and unhurried, moved through the room like a river of devotion.

"*O Gott, Vater, wir loben dich*," she sang. O God, Father, we praise thee.

As the hymn continued, Anika felt the ache in her chest ease. The grief that had silenced her for so long loosened its grip. These were the hymns her mother had sung, and her grandmother before her, prayers woven into sound, passed down through the years. The words of praise offered comfort.

A good long while had passed since she'd sat among these people—her *kinner*, her *freinden*—and yet, no one demanded answers. No one pressed. Nor did they need to. In a community where everyone had lost someone, silence was its own kind of compassion.

Today's message, delivered by Abram Mueller, had moved her. He'd spoken of showing up, even when broken. As she listened, the words touched her deeply. It was as if he knew what was in her heart and spoke it aloud.

When she'd invited Elam, she hadn't known his brother would be preaching. After Abram arrived, the two men stepped outside. No one knew what was said between them, but when they'd come back, all seemed calm.

Wondering how Elam was holding up, she glanced across the room. He sat with the men, as was custom. He held his songbook, but it remained closed. He wasn't singing. Instead, he stood still, eyes closed, head slightly bowed. His posture wasn't one of defiance, but reverence, humble and searching. She hadn't seen that look on many people, much less on someone with a past like his.

That isn't something a man can fake.

He might not know the Lord, but he was open to listening. And that was an encouraging start.

As the hymn faded, the congregation kept their places. Then, with the soft rustle of dresses and the creak of wooden benches, the people began to disperse.

A deacon collected the prayer books. "I'll take that, please."

Fingers brushing the worn leather, Anika handed hers over. "*Danke.*" She watched as he placed it on top of the growing stack. Soon, the books would be tucked into a wooden chest and sent along to the next household to host Sunday service.

The peaceful hush gave way to conversation and the shuffle of feet as hungry folks glanced toward the kitchen. The potluck meal was a cherished tradition where food and fellowship wove the final threads of the day's worship into something tangible. Plates would be passed, laughter shared and burdens quietly lifted with the support of friends, which was the best part of the service.

For Anika, it was a step back into a life she had almost forgotten how to love.

"Will you help?" Naomi asked, carrying her infant.

Anika nodded. "Of course."

In the kitchen, the other women had already begun to gather. Each had brought a favorite dish. It was how it had always been. Everyone offered what they could, so the burden would never fall solely on the host.

"Anika!" called Mary Beth Stoltz, her face flushed from the warmth of the stove. "It's so *gut* to see you."

"I heard you've been getting out more," said Hannah Zook, her belly round beneath her apron. She hugged Anika. "We've been praying for you."

Anika smiled. "*Danke.* That means a lot."

"You're looking well," said Katie Ann Boller. "Better than I've seen you look in a long time."

Pulling away, Anika laughed. "I'm feeling better."

More women joined the growing circle around her. They were all close in age, many already married, most with at least one child in their arms or growing beneath their hearts. And yet, despite the differences in their paths, they welcomed her like she'd never been away.

"So, is it true?" asked Diana Lapp, her voice low and curious. "Elam Mueller's working at the farm now?"

"He is," Anika replied. "The bishop sent him to help out, to work off his community service."

Katie Ann clucked her tongue. "*Ach*, that was some terrible business, what happened to Nathan. He could've been killed, the poor *boi*."

Anika stilled. "It wasn't all Elam's fault. Nathan shouldn't have been out that night. He snuck out of the house to go into town, and no one knew where he was. If he hadn't been there, it might never have happened."

Katie Ann's brows shot up. "Well, that's a surprise," she said. "Didn't think I'd hear you defending someone like him. Everyone knows Elam's no *gut*. Even his own family washed their hands of him."

Anika opened her mouth, but she never got the chance to speak.

"That's not true," came a steady voice.

Every head turned.

Maddie Mueller, Abram's *fraa*, stood just inside the doorway, her expression composed but unmistakably firm. By the look on her face, she'd caught every word.

"Elam was never disowned," she continued. "He's the one who pulled away. But that doesn't mean we closed the door. He's welcome home anytime he chooses to come."

Katie Ann flushed. "Well, that's just what I'd heard..."

"You heard wrong," Maddie countered, speaking with the authority of a preacher's wife who had no patience for idle rumors. Silence rippled through the group. The air was heavy with tension.

Naomi stepped between them. "Now, girls, let's remember that Scripture says the words of a talebearer cut like a knife."

Boppli in her arms, her gaze moved to each woman in turn. "As long as Elam behaves with respect, he's welcome in my home. And I hope he'd be welcome in yours, too."

Maddie nodded. "*Danke*, Naomi." Then she turned to the others, her voice carrying more steel than softness. "You would each do well to remember that we're all human. Every one of us. We all stumble. Elam's made choices we might not agree with, but that's no reason to cast him out. We can choose forgiveness. And maybe we can help him grow enough to want to come back to our community." Her gaze sharpened. "As it stands now, the way you hens cluck and peck would scare anyone away."

A few murmurs of apology rippled through the circle, barely more than whispers.

"I didn't mean anything by it," one woman said, glancing down at her hands.

"*Ja*, maybe we were a bit harsh," Katie Ann admitted.

Naomi offered a gentle nod. "We'd best tend to getting the food on the table. We've got hungry men and *youngies* to feed."

Gradually, the clink of dishes and rustle of aprons replaced the tension, and the women returned to preparing the meal.

Still, curiosity lingered.

Anika moved to the counter to sort paper plates and cups.

Diana Lapp sidled up. "So, how well do you know Elam?"

Anika shrugged. "Not well. But he's respectful, and he's a hard worker."

"You think he's changed?"

Anika hesitated. There was a time when she wouldn't have given Elam the benefit of the doubt. But after spending so much time in his company, she saw something steadier, more sincere.

"I think he's trying, and that counts for something."

Lydia Bontrager giggled, leaning closer with a conspiratorial grin. "He's cute. Why, if he were Amish again, I know the girls would be lining up to walk about with him."

Jealousy flickered. She hadn't expected other girls to take

a fancy to Elam. But they had. He was tall and lean, his broad shoulders squared, his wavy hair clipped short in a way that made him look even more striking. Anyone with eyes could see he was handsome. But it was more than that. He carried himself with confidence, a strength that drew attention without trying.

"I'm not sure he'd be interested in that sort of thing," she said, flustered by the rise in her emotions.

Diana leaned closer. "He's not interested?" she echoed. "Or is it that you don't want anyone else to be interested?" There was a hint of jealousy in her voice. A few years older and already considered a spinster, Diana had made no secret of her desire to find a match. She wasn't ugly, just plain in a way that didn't catch a boy's eye. And she knew it, which made her even more determined.

"You think I want Elam?" Anika countered, shaking her head. "*Nein.* Don't be silly."

Clearly unconvinced, Lydia's brows lifted. "You sure? Because it sounded like you were talking him up."

"I'm sure," she said, forcing a laugh. "He's a *freund.* That's all."

Even as the words left her lips, a quiet flutter stirred inside. Just a *freund*? She wanted that to be true. Needed it to be. Because anything else was far too soon. She still carried the ache of loss. There was no room for new feelings right now.

And yet there was something about Elam. The way his eyes softened when he looked at her. The quiet strength in his presence. She couldn't deny the attraction, but it was too much, too fast.

"*Ach,*" Diana muttered. "So much for my chances." Annoyed, she turned and flounced off.

Lydia chuckled. "Looks like you dashed Diana's hopes for an *ehemann.*"

Anika flushed. "I did no such thing," she murmured, turning back to her task. She didn't dare let Lydia see her face.

I don't have feelings for Elam.

At least, that's what she kept telling herself.

Chapter Twelve

"Been a long time since I've been to a hoedown," Elam said. "I didn't know they were still a thing."

Guiding the horse with a steady hand, Anika grinned from the driver's seat. "You've been missing out. They're some of the best fun."

"I don't remember them being that way when I was on *rumspringa*." Elam adjusted his straw hat as the buggy clattered over a covered bridge and onto a rutted trail. "If it gets boring, promise me we'll head back."

Her smile widened. "It won't be," she said as the buggy rolled toward its destination. "Just wait and see."

Elam leaned back against the worn seat, folding his arms. Truth be told, his *rumspringa* was a bust. He'd found the Amish gatherings awkward. Everyone stood in tight groups, whispering and sneaking glances at the opposite sex. Deciding that wasn't his scene, he'd drifted toward his *Englisch* friends instead, fixing up junk cars, cruising the strip, and blasting heavy metal. That had felt more like freedom. More like fun.

Or at least, it used to.

Somewhere along the way, his perspective had changed. Since Anika had agreed to let him help on the farm, a routine had taken shape. Chores in the morning, volunteer work in the afternoon and evenings spent just hanging out and visiting. Joined by Reuben and Nathan, they played board games or had meandering conversations about life, loss and things that mattered. Without quite meaning to, the Glicks had become a kind of makeshift family, one he hadn't realized he'd needed.

I came because she asked, he thought, cutting a glance toward Anika.

His pulse quickened. Hers wasn't the kind of beauty that begged for attention, but it did linger in a man's memory. Fine-boned and willowy, she moved with an unstudied elegance, completely unaware of the impression she left behind.

He liked her. And he liked being near her.

Still, a few weeks wasn't nearly enough time to rush into declaring anything. But if showing up meant he could steal more time with her, then maybe it was worth enduring an evening with other Plain folks their age. Things might get a little boring, but he supposed he'd survive.

"Almost there," Anika said. Sensing the presence of other horses ahead, Mossie whinnied and picked up to a trot. The buggy bounced over ruts in the road, jostling the passengers.

Elam straightened. Just ahead, the narrow track dipped toward a quiet bend, known simply as Burk's Crossing. Tucked amid a thick gathering of trees, the clearing offered a sandy bank where folks could splash in the pond. It sat on private land owned by an Amish widower known for his generosity. The old man didn't mind visitors using the spot so long as they respected it, kept things peaceful, and left no litter behind. Over the years, the place had become a beloved retreat for Amish youth, a haven where they could kick up their heels, laugh a little louder, and enjoy the simple pleasures that summer evenings were made for.

As their buggy rolled closer, Elam's brows lifted in surprise. At least a dozen were already parked beneath the trees, their horses grazing peacefully in the shade. A lively gathering was underway, with blankets and quilts spread across the grass, forming the base of an impromptu picnic. Laughter floated on the breeze, mingling with the crackle of a campfire set near the water's edge.

Anika guided the horse to a stop. Setting the parking brake, she slid the side door open and stepped down.

Elam followed, adjusting his hat as he took in the scene. Since he hadn't had time to go home and change, he'd taken off his jacket and rolled up the sleeves of his shirt to make it more comfortable. The small adjustments made his stiff, formal outfit more comfortable. Still dressed in their Sunday clothes, other Amish men had done the same thing.

The moment their feet hit the ground, a chorus of familiar voices greeted them.

"Anika!" several girls called out.

Anika's face lit up. "*Ach*, it's so *gut* to see all of you!" She moved from one friend to the next, exchanging quick hugs and clasped hands, her laughter mingling with theirs.

"You've been missed," one of the girls said, looping an arm around her shoulders. The two girls began to talk, smiling as they launched into an animated conversation.

Unwilling to step on Anika's moment, Elam hung back. Gaze scraping the crowd, he recognized most of the faces. Many were friends he'd cut loose because they'd stayed in the church, and he had not. *Rumspringa* didn't come with a deadline. Some young adults chose to remain unbaptized well into their adult years, unsure about fully committing to the authority of the church. In the meantime, they might live semi-independently, work *Englisch* jobs, drive cars and sample the wider world, all while keeping a foothold in their community.

"Elam, is that you?" one man asked, straw hat tipped back on his head, dark brows raised. His voice held no malice, just honest curiosity.

Recognition kicked in. The man was Malachi Schrock. A familiar figure around town, he ran the local Chamber of Commerce, helping Plain folks navigate the requirements of doing business in the *Englisch* world. An older man, he was the unofficial gatekeeper and guardian of the peace. Malachi made sure everyone behaved themselves. A good time was permitted, even expected. But there were rules, and everyone knew them: No alcohol. No drugs. And no funny business.

"*Ja*," Elam said, slipping into *Deitsch*. "I hope you don't mind me showing up. I know it's been a while…and I guess the gossip has gotten around that I got in trouble."

Malachi's allowed a knowing smile. "I don't think there's anyone who doesn't know. Word around is Bishop Graber took you in hand and is trying to set you back on the straight path."

"That he is. Don't know if the path is exactly straight, but I'm walking it the best I can."

"I was glad to see you in church this morning." Malachi's gaze moved across the clearing. "And Anika, too. She looks so much better, happier. After Ada and Jason passed, everyone tried to help, but she closed herself off. We worried for her."

"Well," Elam said, glancing toward the group of girls Anika had joined. "I think she just needed to work through things. The bishop asked me to be a friend, and I've been trying."

Malachi's expression grew thoughtful. "I'm glad. Life's too short to live it shut away." He gave Elam a firm pat on the back. "It's nice to see both of you."

"Danke."

"Come, join us." Malachi stepped aside with a welcoming sweep of his arm. "There's plenty for all."

Elam gave Malachi a nod and then followed him toward the group. A campfire blazed near the pond's edge, the flames dancing high as dry wood popped and crackled. Smoke curled lazily upward into the darkening sky, where the first stars were beginning to blink through the haze of twilight.

Firelight flickered across familiar faces. Laughter bubbled up, light and familiar, blending with the chirp of crickets and the soft splash of water as someone skipped a rock across the pond.

"Well, look what the wind blew in," Gideon Lapp said, grinning.

"It's been too long," Lamar Raber drawled.

Elam nodded, his smile widening despite himself. "Guess I figured it was time to see what everyone was up to on the Plain side."

Malachi grabbed two sodas from a cooler nestled nearby. "You know I'm here just to keep an eye on these two," he said, watching the pair.

Gideon smirked. "Hey now, I'm reformed. Mostly."

Lamar laughed. "He's still living down the 'Lizzy incident.'"

Elam looked between them. "Do I want to know?"

"Oh, it was a real fine moment," Malachi drawled. "Last time we were out here, Gideon got it in his head to flirt with my Lizzy. Told her she had 'eyes like dew' or some such nonsense."

Gideon held up a hand. "It was poetic."

"She said it was creepy," Lamar said, grinning. "Next thing we know, Lizzy shoved him right into the pond, boots and all."

"I had just filled my plate," Gideon muttered, pretending offense. "Lost two hot dogs and a slice of shoofly pie."

"You deserved it," Malachi said, grinning. "My daughter doesn't suffer fools gladly."

"I'll talk her into marrying me yet," Gideon declared with a dramatic sigh.

"We'll see," Malachi muttered, his tone dry but not unkind. "In the meantime, you boys behave, and don't be dragging Elam into any of your shenanigans."

Elam relaxed. The warmth of belonging reached past his doubt and settled somewhere deep. "I promise, I'll have nothing to do with it," he said, twisting the cap off his soda before taking a drink.

The men continued their conversation, exchanging jokes and playful jabs that made the night feel like something out of a simpler time.

Half listening to the banter, Elam's gaze drifted toward

Anika. She stood near the edge of the clearing, laughing with her friends. Seeing her like that stirred something hopeful deep inside him, a subtle lift to his mood he hadn't expected.

What would it be like to court her? To walk beside her under the vast evening sky, sharing whispered talks and dreams…

He shook his head, blinking to clear the unfamiliar thoughts. He hadn't ever seen himself as the kind who'd want a *fraa* or *kinder.* At least not right away, not until he had his own business established and his life on track.

But now he wasn't so sure.

What's going on with me?

The question nagged as he moved to stand near the fire, his bottle of cola forgotten in his hand. The chatter around him continued, but it went unheard. Something inside him was veering in a direction he hadn't anticipated. Maybe it was being back among familiar faces, folks he knew and had grown up with. Maybe it was the slow work of time, loss and lessons learned. Or maybe it was God guiding him forward. Not in loud, unmistakable ways, but in soft nudges tucked inside ordinary events.

Mind spinning, Elam drew in a sharp breath. He didn't have everything figured out, not by a long shot. But he could sense a change in his old habits as new ones began to emerge. The feckless youth he'd been was giving way to someone new—a man more responsible and mature. Somehow, being around Anika brought out the best in him.

A lump rose in his throat as the truth settled over him. He wanted to be with her.

Don't be foolish, he warned himself. But it didn't feel that way. It felt right.

He shook his head. Was this what being in love felt like? The feeling wasn't anything like the surge of adrenaline he used to chase. This was something else entirely.

And it terrified him.

* * *

From the corner of her eye, Anika caught sight of Elam standing near the campfire, a little apart from the other men gathered around. Though he laughed and took an occasional sip of his soft drink, he looked like he wasn't quite a part of the conversation. Subdued and contained, he was present but not exactly participating.

"Keep staring like that and you'll twist your neck plumb off," Hannah Zook said with a grin.

Anika startled and looked away quickly. "Sorry," she mumbled.

Beside her, Katie Ann Boller laughed and gave Anika a gentle elbow. "You haven't taken your eyes off him since we arrived."

Anika's face heated. "I didn't realize I was looking."

Arms folded, Mary Beth Stoltz leaned in. "He's certainly reformed himself. Not the trouble he used to be, for sure."

"I don't trust him," Diana Lapp said, her tone sharp. "He'll head right back to the *Englisch* the moment his community service is up. Showing up to service today? That was just for appearances."

Katie Ann blinked. "How do you know?"

Diana gave a tight-lipped smile. "If he truly believed, he never would've walked away from our community." Her voice grew colder. "I think he's putting on a big act."

"I don't think that's true," Anika said.

All eyes turned to her.

"And just what do you think?" Diana demanded, smirking.

Anika drew a breath. Having spent most of the last few weeks with Elam, she hadn't detected anything insincere or deceptive in his manner. Far from it. Since arriving at the farm, he'd gone out of his way to get the work done, even doing things he wasn't asked to, like fixing the front gate and reorganizing the cluttered shed. But what stood out most was how he treated her father. Elam didn't look at Reuben with pity or avoid him like some folks did. He talked to him straight, with respect, and made a real effort to include him, asking for his input on repairs, checking in with him about tools, even wheeling him out to the barn so he could see how things were coming along.

"He wouldn't be here at all if he didn't want to be," she said. "People don't pretend like that when no one's asking them to."

"I believe everyone deserves a chance to make amends," Lizzy Schrock said, speaking up for the first time. A shy, soft-spoken girl with frizzy brown hair, thick glasses, and a noticeable overbite, she wasn't conventionally pretty, but there was something gentle and genuine about her that made people look twice. Something that lingered.

Anika glanced toward her friend. When others had urged her to shake off her grief and move on, it was Lizzy who told her it was okay to take her time, to feel every bit of it until her heart caught up with her mind.

"*Danke*," she said, grateful someone else had spoken up on Elam's behalf. "He might have a bad reputation, but he's trying to redeem himself."

"I'll believe that when I see him on his knees begging *Gott* for forgiveness," Diana replied with a sniff.

Lizzy calmly pushed her glasses up the bridge of her nose. "And how do you know he hasn't?"

"I know enough," Diana muttered.

"No," Lizzy said, "you know what you've settled in your mind. What you've assumed. And you know what they say about folks who do that."

Diana's lips tightened into a scowl. "Why I never—" she spluttered.

Lizzy's expression didn't change, but there was quiet fire behind her words. "Oh, yes, you do," she scolded, waggling a finger. "If Elam's trying to change, the last thing he needs is people tearing him down."

Anika nodded. "We don't get to decide who is worthy," she

added. "That's *Gott*'s job. Ours is to love, even when it's hard. Especially when it's hard."

Flustered by being called out, Diana let out a sharp breath. "Fine," she snapped. "You go right on admiring him. See how far that gets you." With a dramatic whirl of her skirt, she turned on her heel and stalked off, leaving a heavy silence in her wake.

Katie Ann let out a low whistle. "And she wonders why the fellows all turn the other way when they see her coming."

Before any more could be said, Malachi's deep voice rang out from near the fire.

"Girls! Bring the food. Don't let us starve out here!"

That set off laughter and teasing shouts, and the girls hurried to fetch and deliver the feast. Tables had been set up earlier under the edge of the trees, covered in simple cloths. It wasn't a formal setting, but the kind of relaxed gathering meant for fellowship, music and maybe a bit of quiet courtship.

Anika helped carry foil-wrapped trays of hot dogs and skewers toward the snapping campfire. The smell of firewood drifted upward in the warm June air, mingling with the faint scent of pine needles.

She was eager to be here, back among friends, craving the easy companionship and laughter of the community. Still, a strange hollow sensation tugged at her heart. Jason wasn't here anymore. The space her brother once occupied felt like a weight she couldn't shake. She remembered how he'd watched Lizzie Schrock from a distance, too shy to say much, but interested enough to keep looking. The way he stole glances at Malachi's daughter, full of hopeful hesitation, had led her to nudge her brother toward declaring his intentions.

But he'd never gotten the chance.

Nothing ventured, nothing gained.

Anika's gaze drifted toward Elam, standing near the fire. The glow softened his face, and without really meaning to, she found herself wondering what life might be like if he were there beside her, not with words or promises, but simply in companionship. A gentle presence to share the days ahead, easing the loneliness she often felt. The thought settled within her, as delicate and uncertain as the flickering flames, yet somehow comforting.

She turned away, biting back the longing.

He's not Amish, she reminded herself. Nor had he given any sign that he intended to return to the Plain community once his court-ordered time was completed.

Malachi's cheerful voice cut through her thoughts. "All right, everyone, grab your hot dogs and skewers."

One by one, hands reached eagerly toward the trays, claiming their simple fare to roast over the glowing campfire. Laughter bubbled up as the group gathered close, the crackling flames casting flickering shadows on their faces. Occasionally, a frank slipped from a skewer, plopping into the embers with a soft sizzle, sending a curl of smoke spiraling skyward.

Despite these mishaps, the warmth of the fire and the easy camaraderie wrapped around them like a comforting blanket. The humble meal was savored by all, each bite a pleasure.

Enjoying everyone's company, Anika felt the heavy ache of her brother's absence lift, replaced by the gentle solace of shared laughter and familiar faces. The calm evening flowed effortlessly, conversation rising and falling, punctuated by bursts of laughter and the soft twinkle of fireflies blinking over the still waters of the pond.

As the last s'more was toasted and the sky deepened to full night, Gideon Lapp produced his banjo, fingers dancing across the strings. Lamar Raber followed, coaxing a gentle tune from his fiddle. A harmonica joined in, its bluesy notes weaving through the air.

Then, with the band fully assembled, the true spirit of the hoedown ignited as the familiar, toe-tapping strains of "Turkey in the Straw" filled the air. Soon, the girls around the fire were clapping in time, their smiles bright in the firelight, as the music carried them into a night of joyful celebration.

Anika closed her eyes, the melody pulling her into a memory. Jason had once sat among them, his fingers strumming with ease and his heart full of hope. He'd loved music more than anything and had dreamed of moving to Nashville to become a gospel singer. He'd believed *Gott* had given him that gift for a reason.

Now, he'd never get the chance to find out.

Her throat tightened. The ache of missing her brother hadn't eased. It simply changed shape, slipping into discreet moments like this one.

From across the gathering, Lamar paused in his banjo playing and called out, "Hey, Elam! We need some percussion. You still play the spoons?"

Elam blinked, startled. "Not in a long while."

"That doesn't mean you forgot how," Lamar said with a grin.

"Come on," Katie Ann urged, holding up a pair of old metal spoons. "Play like you used to."

Laughter and teasing encouragement rippled through the group as Elam stood, sheepish but smiling, shaking his head as though he couldn't quite believe he was going along with it.

"All right, all right," he said, accepting the spoons. Sitting on a nearby log, he adjusted the angle of the set in one hand, curved back-to-back, their rounded bowls facing outward. Holding the handles lightly between his fingers, he rested one spoon against his thigh and hovered the other just above it. "Haven't done this in years," he muttered, testing a few tentative clicks against his leg.

"It'll come back," Malachi said, encouraging him to try.

Elam began again. The sound came—uneven at first—but soon his fingers found the rhythm. The spoons clicked and bounced, tapping against his leg and the palm of his opposite hand in quick succession. His wrist flicked in practiced movements, alternating low strikes against his thigh with sharp taps against his other hand, building a rhythm both playful and precise.

The banjo jumped back in, followed closely by the fiddle, and the music lifted. The beat Elam set was clever and lively, full of unexpected syncopations that made people laugh and clap along.

Anika clapped, too, her hands keeping rhythm almost without thinking. Before she knew it, the fire, the music and the laughter all felt natural again.

The music slowed as the players paused for a rest.

"Anika, how about a song?" Katie Ann called.

She blinked, caught off guard. "Why—I don't know."

Mary Beth leaned in. "You should."

"You have a fine voice," Malachi prodded gently. "It's only right to lift it in praise."

Now that all eyes were on her, she couldn't say no.

Slowly, Anika rose, smoothing her apron. Drawing a steadying breath, she tilted her gaze toward the vast stretch of velvet above her head. Then she opened her mouth and began to sing the first lines of a familiar hymn she'd known since childhood.

"Even in sorrow, my prayers will rise…"

At that line, something inside her broke open. Not with pain, but with praise.

The fire popped. No one spoke.

Lifting her voice, Anika felt it. Not just sorrow, but love. Not only grief, but grace.

Not only remembering those she'd lost but cherishing those she'd gained.

And, above all, trusting that *Gott* still had more reasons for her to sing…

Chapter Thirteen

Elam walked beside Anika, their footsteps muffled by the packed earth of the trail. The voices and laughter faded behind them as the crickets started their nightly song. Fireflies flickered over the tall grass near the pond, their light soft and playful. A full moon hung over the trees, casting silvery slivers across the surface of the water.

"Thanks again for inviting me," he said, breaking the quiet between them. "I had a great day."

"Church and all?"

He glanced sideways. The moonlight softened the lines of her face, catching on the edge of her slightly askew *kapp*. "Church and all. I didn't realize how long it had been since…" He hesitated, the rest snagging in his throat. "Since I let myself miss it."

Anika smiled, her gaze never quite meeting his. "I was worried you'd find it boring."

"Not even close. I enjoyed the service." Grinning, he added, "And I haven't played the spoons in years, but it was fun. Didn't think I could anymore."

"You're *gut* at it," she said, brushing a hand along the tall grass lining the path. "Jason would've loved playing with you. He was always looking for someone who could keep up with his rhythm."

"I'm sorry I missed the chance to play with him."

"Me, too." Her voice turned quiet. "He dreamed of playing the Grand Ole Opry someday."

"An Amish boy on the Opry stage. That would've been something to see."

"*Mamm* didn't think so. Said chasing attention was going against *Gottes wille*."

Elam paused. "I don't think the ambition to entertain is selfish."

"It was hard for him," she explained. "He loved *Gott* and wanted to play for His glory. But being Plain, he didn't get much encouragement. He wasn't baptized, so he still had the right to choose. Sometimes *Mamm* and *Daed* argued about it."

"Do you think he would've left the community?"

Teeth grazing her lower lip, Anika hesitated. "Maybe. For a little while. I think he wanted to see what the world was like. But deep down?" Her gaze dropped. "I don't think he'd stay away forever. He loved his home."

Home.

The word settled heavily in Elam's gut. He had a place to sleep at night, a roof over his head. But a real home, a place where he belonged, was a memory that grew dimmer with each passing year.

He used to have one. He could still see the wood smoke curling from the chimney on a chilly morning, smell his *mamm*'s cinnamon bread cooling on the kitchen counter. He remembered the way his *daed*'s laughter used to roll through the house like distant thunder, how his older siblings would race to greet him after school and chores were done for the day. There had been warmth, noise, even arguments.

Now? He had nothing like that.

A knot tightened in his throat. He hadn't let himself think about it in so long, but now that he had, the ache was undeniable. He wanted it again. Not just a place to throw his clothes and stretch out, but a home. Somewhere to land. Someone waiting. But having it seemed impossibly out of his reach.

Conversation falling to silence, they walked on.

Their steps settled into an easy rhythm, the crunch of gravel beneath their feet a quiet counterpoint to the distant murmur of voices.

Arriving at the far edge of the pond, Elam paused, looking out over the water. It was still except for the occasional ripple where a frog or fish stirred. Somewhere far off, an owl called into the night.

"Now, don't be going out of sight!" Malachi Schrock yelled from behind, his voice sharp as a whip crack.

Elam glanced over his shoulder. Malachi stood like a sentry at the edge of the clearing, arms folded across his chest, eyes scanning the couples with the intensity of a hawk circling prey. As a chaperone, he took his job of keeping an eye on young folks seriously. A fella might sneak a smooch or squeeze a hand if he was bold, but that was all Malachi ever allowed. Any more than that wasn't going to happen on his watch.

"I'd forgotten how strict things can get," he said, shaking his head.

"Don't let Malachi fool you," Anika laughed. "Now that Lizzy's of age, he's anxious for her to find a proper beau to walk about with."

Elam raised a brow. "That man looks like he'd chase off every boy from here to Kalamazoo."

She rolled his eyes. "Oh, he would. But only the ones who don't measure up."

"Sounds like Lizzy's going to be an old maid before she finds anyone."

"Her *daed* means well. He's just trying to keep things decent. No surprise *rumspringa bopplin* are happening under his watch."

Aware that other eyes watched, Elam shoved his hands in his pockets. "It's funny," he said after a beat. "Being here, around all this again, has made me think about everything I left behind. My family. This community. All of it."

Anika glanced over, curiosity flickering in her gaze. "Do you ever think about coming back?"

"More often than I'd like to admit." He let out a slow breath. "But it's not that simple as saying I'd like to and then doing it."

"Why not?"

Elam bent to pick up a flat stone, its surface worn smooth by years of rain and river. He turned it over in his hand, slow and thoughtfully. "It was hard for me, living by all the rules," he admitted, his fingers brushing the edges. "What I could do, what I couldn't. It felt like I couldn't breathe." He let the stone fly. It skimmed the water once, twice, and then disappeared beneath the surface.

Yeah, he thought. *That's exactly it.* That's how he felt. Pulled under by expectations he'd never agreed to. But now, he was older. And what had once felt suffocating at eighteen didn't seem unreasonable at twenty-two. The *Ordnung* hadn't changed much since he'd walked away.

However, he had.

Beside him, Anika visually followed the ripple where the stone had disappeared.

"Our district isn't as strict as some," she reminded. "We're allowed phones, for business and emergency purposes. Some even have electricity in their homes when there's a medical need. And Bishop Graber does listen. If the *Leit* agrees, he's open to change. The church is moving into a real meetinghouse. And he did approve buying a van for folks who can't use buggies. That doesn't sound so suffocating to me."

He glanced at her. "Not when you say it like that."

She angled her head. "Then what's holding you back?"

"Honestly? I'm still trying to work things out with God. Trying to understand where He fits into everything. Sometimes I wonder if He still speaks to people the way He used to."

Anika moved slightly, the gravel crunching beneath her boots. "He is speaking. We've just forgotten how to listen."

She hugged her arms across her chest, not in defiance but as if holding herself together. "I know I did. After the accident, I was scared and angry. But blaming *Gott* felt easier than trusting Him."

Elam looked at her, this girl who had lost so much and still found the courage to believe. She'd reached for faith, even when it had let her down.

"Yet you found your way back."

"I have."

"How?"

A breeze tugged at the loose strands of hair around her face. She absently brushed the strands aside. "Because when life falls apart, someone has to be there to put the pieces back together," she replied. "*Gott* can do that. He showed me, and I believe it. With all my heart." There was something unshakable in the simplicity of her words.

Elam pursed his lips. "I'd like to be able to. I really would. But I'm still trying to make sense of it all."

Anika nodded. She didn't press. The understanding between them held space for grace.

Boot scuffing the ground, he looked toward the dark horizon. "My community service ends next week." The time for drifting was nearly over. Soon, he'd have to choose his path and follow it.

Anika's expression dimmed. "You must be happy about that."

He hesitated. "Not really."

"Why not?"

"I like helping out at the farm," he said. "There's still so much to do, and leaving wouldn't sit right with me."

"Is that so?"

"Yeah. It is," he said. "And there's your dad. I admire Reuben. He's been through a lot, but he's grounded in his beliefs in a way I can't even begin to imagine. I've seen how he holds things together. Not just for you and Nathan, but for everyone around him. There's a kind of peace in him."

"*Daed*'s always been strong in the Word," she said. "Even though his body is broken, he's never given up hope."

"I know." Elam grinned. "And then there's Nathan. That kid's something else. I would've liked having a little brother like him. I was the youngest, you know. My older siblings didn't always include me. They were off doing things, and I kind of got left behind."

"Is that why you got into mechanics?"

"Yeah," he said. "*Mamm* wanted to keep me busy while she did housework, so she let me hang around the *Englisch* handyman who came by to fix stuff on the property. I started out handing him tools, then eventually he let me help with simple repairs. I liked the way machines made sense. If something was broken, there was usually a way to fix it."

Anika smiled. "Everyone's still talking about how happy the pastor was when you fixed the delivery van. He was worried nobody would get their meals that day. But you figured it out like it was nothing."

Embarrassed by the praise, Elam ducked his head. "He asked me if I wanted to keep volunteering once the judge cuts me loose."

Her brow lifted. "Are you going to?"

He shrugged, shifting his weight. "Don't know. I'm waiting to see how things shake out with, uh, other details."

Anika's smile turned curious. "Other details?"

Daring a glance at her, his pulse kicked up. "Yeah. That would be—um—you."

"Me?"

"I like you," he blurted, the words rough and honest. "A lot."

Surprised, she blinked. "You do?"

He looked at her, hope settling in that place where his emotions had once gone still. "Yeah. And I'd like to get to know you better." His pulse pounded in his ears, but he pushed the words out anyway.

She gave him a playful nudge. "Please, don't tease."

"I'm not," he breathed, stepping closer.

A hush settled around them. Above, the stars blinked against the velvet folds of night. The pond shimmered beneath the moonlight, and the trees whispered in the gentle night breeze.

Elam wondered if he'd crossed the line, revealing too much too soon. But then her expression softened, abandoning its edge of wariness.

Taking a chance, he leaned in. "May I…kiss you?"

Her answering smile bloomed warm and sure. "I thought you would never ask."

He moved closer—slowly, giving her every chance to pull away.

She didn't. Instead, she met him halfway.

Their lips met in a way that was soft and tentative. Not a claim, but a question. An unspoken potential wrapped in the sweet promises of youth and the possibility of what tomorrow might bring.

Anika stepped through the front door, the familiar creak of the hinges giving her away before she could even slip off her shoes. The house was dark except for the warm, flickering glow coming from the lamp in the sitting room. She didn't have to guess who had waited up.

"*Daed*?" she called, setting her boots by the bench in the foyer.

"In here."

She smoothed the front of her dress, suddenly aware of the giddy flutter still dancing in her chest. The evening had felt like a dream, a warm, music-laced dream that had ended with Elam's lips gently brushing hers beneath a starlit sky. Her cheeks warmed all over again just remembering it.

Drawing a calming breath, she stepped into the sitting room. Of course, her father had waited up. She hadn't meant to stay out so late, but after the cookout, she'd needed to drive Elam home, dropping him off at his garage apartment. He'd invited her in to hang out and have a soda, but she'd declined.

Daed sat in his wheelchair, a crocheted afghan folded neatly over his knees. Lowering the book he'd been reading, he looked tired, with faint lines of strain around his eyes. His mouth lifted in a small smile as she entered the room.

"You should have gone to bed," she said, walking over and draping her shawl on the back of an armchair.

Affection touched his smile. "A *vater* needs to know his daughter is home safe, especially when it's so late."

"Oh, it's just a little past eleven. Not late at all."

Closing his book, *Daed* laid it in his lap. "Enough for Nathan to be in bed," he replied, tipping his head to glance at her over the rims of his reading glasses. "He turned in just after evening prayers."

Anika smiled. She knew she'd stayed out longer than she should have. But the cookout had been so lively, so full of laughter and music and stories, it was hard to say goodbye. Still, come ten o'clock, Malachi Schrock had clapped his hands and declared the evening over. The food was packed up, the campfire extinguished, and folks were sent on their way.

She sank into the chair across from him, folding her hands in her lap to keep from fidgeting. "I'm sorry." Brightening, she added, "I hope you had a *gut* visit with *Mammi* and *Poppi* today."

"We did. Had a quiet Bible study and sat out after supper for a while. They were glad to hear you're going to church again."

"The service was a fine one," she said. "Jacob and Naomi Mishler hosted, and I got to see their new baby. She's such a sweet little thing. Oh, and Abram Mueller did the preaching."

"I know," *Daed* said, offering a little smile. "Matter of fact, Abram dropped by to ask how Elam was working out."

Surprise filled her. "Did he?"

"Mmm-hmm," *Daed* affirmed. "He said Elam was respectful and stayed for the whole service."

"That's true. He seemed to enjoy it."

"Abram also said Lizzy Schrock invited you to her gathering, and not to expect you home early."

Anika nodded. Though *Daed* didn't use a phone, news still traveled fast in the small community. "I didn't see any reason not to go."

"Elam went too, I suppose?"

"*Ja.* A lot of young single folks were there. And Malachi kept an eye, as he always does."

"Malachi's a *gut* man. I trust him to keep things proper."

"He did."

Daed gave her a moment, watching her with the attentiveness of a man who knew more than he said. "How was the cookout?"

Anika leaned back, eyes drifting toward the ceiling as the evening unfolded again in her mind. "It was lovely. We roasted hot dogs over the campfire, and the boys brought out their instruments to play. Elam joined in, too."

"I hope no one had any problem with him showing up," *Daed* commented. "He's been gone a long time."

"Everyone was kind. Elam even played the spoons. You should've heard him. He's incredibly talented. Jason would've gotten such a kick out of it. They would've made quite the pair." She hesitated, then smiled softly. "And I sang. In front of everyone. Just like I used to."

Surprise filled his eyes. "You did?"

"When I heard the music, I just had to praise the Lord."

Daed's gaze settled on her, full of quiet pride. "I can't tell you what it means to see you finding your voice again. I can hardly believe the change in you. It's been such a blessing, watching you come out of your shell, going back to church, and spending time with your friends."

Her smile faltered. "I didn't do it on my own. *Gott* helped me. More than I can say." She hesitated, then added, "And so did Elam."

Daed tilted his head. "How did he help you, *mei dochder*?"

She looked down for a moment, her fingers fidgeting with the edge of her apron. "He listened," she said finally. "And he didn't rush me or try to fix things. He just showed up."

Daed nodded. "Go on."

"I didn't think it would work out, you know, having Elam around. Not at first. I wasn't sure I could trust him, after everything. But he's nothing like what people said. He's kind. He works hard. And I know he's sorry for what happened."

Daed gave a thoughtful nod. "I don't believe in holding a man forever to a mistake. I was a young man once, too. I remember how hard it was to choose between running wild and following the *Ordnung*. But I grew up. Most young men do, given the chance."

"He says he wants to change." She paused, swallowing past the lump in her throat. "And I believe him."

"Change? In what way?"

"I can't speak for him. But from the things he said tonight, it sounds like he's searching for a way back. Back to the church. Back to *Gott*."

Daed's gaze softened. "If that's true, then it's a blessed thing. There's nothing more powerful than a heart turning back to the Lord."

Anika's gaze drifted to the nearby oil lamp. The dancing flame cast flickering shadows along the walls. The heaviness of an unsaved soul pressed on her chest, perhaps heavier because she cared for Elam more than she dared to admit.

"Given time, I truly believe he'll find his way."

"I'm praying for him," *Daed* said quietly. "And when Elam's ready, Jesus Christ will be there to receive him."

Anika's breath caught, the words sinking deep. "Do you think it's possible, *Daadi*?" she asked, using the tender name she'd called him since childhood.

"Anything's possible," he said. "*Gott* works in ways we can't always see."

"I—I'd like to see Elam come back to the community."

"We all would." His gaze lingered on her, steady and perceptive. Then, almost imperceptibly, his expression softened. A quiet understanding lit his eyes. "*Ach*, so it's like that."

She blinked. "Like what?"

Daed let out a long, low breath. "You've got feelings for the *boi*."

Heat rushed to her face. Her heart skipped a beat, thudding unevenly. Was it that plain?

Should I deny it? Or tell the truth?

Flustered, she said nothing. Unable to look at him, she dropped her gaze.

Silence settled, broken only by the loud tick of the clock on the wall. Each beat echoed the flutter in her chest.

Finally, *Daed* cleared his throat. "*Lieb*, you've only known him a little while."

Anika folded her arms across her stomach, pressing them in as if to hold herself together. "I don't know why I feel this way. I only know I do."

She risked a glance up. Her father's expression was clouded. Not with anger, but with worry. He wasn't judging her. He was protecting her.

"I think I love him," she whispered.

"Is it possible you've confused friendship for something more?" he asked, brow furrowing. "You isolated yourself so long in grief. And then Elam came along and offered you comfort."

"*Nein*. It's not like that."

Daed hesitated. "This is all so sudden." His eyes narrowed, thoughtful. "I don't know what to think."

Anika raised her chin, meeting his gaze. "You always told us you wanted to marry *Mamm* the first day you saw her."

He blinked, surprised. Then a smile tugged at the corner of his mouth, fond, sad and a little resigned. "*Ja*, I did."

"Tell me again how you met her."

Daed leaned back in his chair. "The first time I saw Ada was at a barn raising. She was hauling planks twice her size, barefoot, no less. Hair flying loose, skirt hem torn and a stubborn streak in her a mile wide." He let the memory settle, momentarily stepping back into the past. "I remember thinking she was the most beautiful mess I'd ever seen. And she was mine for twenty-three years."

"Then you know how I feel," she said. "Elam makes me happy."

"And?"

"I want to be with him." As she spoke, warmth stirred in her chest, a tender hope she didn't dare name aloud. She remembered the brush of Elam's lips on hers, the way the world had gone still all around her. Then, it had felt like the beginning of something precious.

Daed's jaw tightened, his lips pressing into a grim line. "You're of age," he agreed. "I won't forbid you. You've a right to choose your path. But this one you're thinking of leads to a hard road." As he spoke, worry shadowed his expression. "Does he know you have feelings?"

She shook her head. "I haven't told him."

Daed nodded, as if confirming something to himself. "We don't always get to choose who we love. Our hearts make that decision for us before we even realize it's happened. But loving someone doesn't always mean you can build a life with them."

Emotion blurred her vision. Was it the worry behind his words or the sorrow beneath them that cut so deeply?

"I'm not trying to hurt you," he said, wheeling closer. "I only want you to be certain. Take this to the Lord in prayer. Ask not for your heart's longing, but for wisdom. You see the man Elam is now. But can you accept the man he might never become? The man who may never return to the community, who may never be baptized?"

His questions hung, heavy and raw.

"I want to believe he will."

"But you don't know?"

Uncertainty pressed hard. "*Nein.*"

Then, softly, *Daed* asked, "What about you, *mei dochder*? Would you leave for him?"

Startled, Anika's head jerked up. "Leave?" she echoed. "Why I—" Her voice faltered. She stared past him, thoughts racing. "I never thought about that."

"You need to."

The innocent pleasure she'd experienced that night evaporated, replaced by the solemn hush of truth too heavy to ignore. "I don't want to choose, not between him and the church." Not between her heart and her soul.

"Then pray. For him, and yourself. Because love isn't only about what we feel. It's about faith. And sometimes, the hardest part of faith of all is learning to let go."

"I will." A tear trickled down her cheek. She brushed it away, but another followed. "I'll ask *Gott* to lead me to the *ehemann* He has planned."

Reaching out, *Daed* gently clasped her hand. "So will I, *mei kind*. So will I."

As his words faded into the quiet of the room, a stillness settled between them, each lost in their own thoughts.

The idea of Elam never returning—of him choosing the *Englisch* world over their way of life—cut deeper than she'd expected. Yet even through the soft ache of longing, she knew she had to release him to *Gott*'s will.

If Elam's path led elsewhere, she would still pray for him. But if it led him home, she would be waiting…

Chapter Fourteen

Reuben sat in his wheelchair, sweat beading on his forehead as he gripped a pair of small dumbbells. His arms trembled with effort, every lift a battle.

Elam crouched beside him, nodding with each curl. "That's it. Nice and slow. Breathe through it."

Reuben let out a short grunt, curling the weights up with a shaky exhale. "Seven..."

"You got it."

"Eight..." The word came through clenched teeth.

"You've gotten this far," Elam said. "Keep going."

"...Nine," Reuben gasped. "Ten." With a grunt, he let the dumbbells drop, arms trembling as he slumped back. His chest rose and fell in rapid breaths. "Thought my arms were going to fall off."

Elam picked up the pair, setting them aside before grabbing a cold bottle of water from the cooler. "Here. You earned this."

Reuben took the bottle with a grateful nod and pressed it to his forehead. But when he tried to lift it for a sip, it slipped from his fingers and hit the ground with a dull thud. "*Ach!*" he muttered, frustrated. "Slipped right out of my hand."

Elam frowned. "Something wrong?"

Reuben flexed his right hand, then rolled his shoulder with a tight grimace. "Just a cramp. Maybe pushed a little too hard."

Elam noticed the way Reuben's fingers curled slightly and

how his shoulder seemed stiffer than usual. "I think you've had enough for today."

"I can do more," Reuben insisted, wincing as he tried to make himself comfortable. "I need to get stronger so I can walk again."

"Don't put the cart before the horse," he insisted. "We can try again tomorrow."

Reuben gave a tired laugh. "I hope you don't feel you have to spend all your time hanging around here. I'm sure there are other things you'd rather be doing."

Elam shrugged, his gaze drifting toward the fence line. "Didn't feel right to just walk away because the judge cut me loose. You gave me more of a chance than I probably deserved. Figured I'd stick around, see things through. Help get you back on your feet."

Reuben's expression softened. "You've done more than just see things through. The truth is, we weren't doing so well before you showed up. Nathan was angry and upset, sneaking out. And Anika…" The older man swallowed hard, his gaze briefly turning toward the house. "She shut down completely. Hid from the world, from her pain. It was beginning to feel like I'd lost all my *youngies*, not just Jason."

"If I'd have known what happened, I'd have come," he said. "I regret not knowing sooner."

"I believe *Gott* works in His own time," Reuben said. "You arrived at the right time, when we all needed you. And things have changed so much. Nathan has stopped acting out. And my daughter—" His voice broke. "I've never seen her smile like she does when you're around. You pulled her back into the light. You gave her a reason to stop mourning and start living." He shook his head in wonder. "That's not just something you do by showing up. That's something only a *gut* man does. Maybe you thought you came too late. But in my mind, you came at exactly the right time."

"I'm just glad to have a place to hang out," he said. "My phone's not exactly ringing a lot lately." He offered a sheepish grin. "Been looking for a job, but nobody's called back." Jace had offered him a job, but flipping burgers wasn't exactly his scene.

"You're a skilled mechanic. I wouldn't think you'd have difficulty finding someone to hire you."

He shrugged again. "Doesn't matter. No one wants to hire the guy who hurt an Amish kid. Word got around. And losing my license made it worse."

"What are you going to do?"

"I've been thinking about what Pastor Jensen said. About working for myself."

Reuben raised a brow. "Yeah?"

"I mean, I've got my garage and my tools. Now I just need to get the word out. Let folks know I'm open for business." Working for himself meant no background checks. No suspicious glances. Just a chance to prove he wasn't the rabble-rouser everyone assumed he was.

"You've already got your first customer, if I'm not mistaken," Rueben said, a knowing smile tugging at his lips.

Elam nodded. The bishop had taken his advice and made the purchase. "Can't believe he talked them down that much." He shook his head, still a little surprised. "Played the charity card, and that appealed to the salesman's better nature."

Rueben chuckled. "James Graber's always had a way of bringing out the best in people."

"I'm just waiting on a few parts," Elam added. "The lift's busted, but it's an easy fix. Once that's done and I give it a tune-up, it'll be good as new."

"I've no doubt the bishop will spread the word once it's running. He's not one to keep quiet when someone does honest work."

"You think he'd recommend me?"

"He always gives credit where it's due. You show him what you're made of, and he'll make sure others see it, too."

Before Elam could answer, a familiar voice called from across the yard.

"Hey, Elam—can you come look at this throttle linkage? It's not lining up right."

Elam glanced across the yard. Sleeves rolled up and hair plastered to his forehead, Nathan was hunched over a jigsaw assembly of bike parts laid out on a tarp. The frame was almost complete now, with the engine mounted and the rear basket welded on.

He'd promised to help the teenager build a new bike, and together they'd spent days combing the junkyard for usable parts. Searching high and low, they'd found the perfect project: a three-wheeled frame with a sturdy carryall basket. An old lawn mower engine would give it the power to go farther and faster. Once finished, the bike would be a unique one-of-a-kind build.

"Let me check on this." Pushing to his feet, he walked over to look at the project.

Nathan barely glanced up. "I can't figure this out," he muttered, wiping sweat from his brow as he squinted at the throttle assembly.

Elam knelt and tugged at the cable. "Throttle cable's binding," he said, tracing the line with his fingers. "Here—see how the housing's kinked?"

Nathan frowned. "Is that what's messing it up?"

"Yeah, it's bent." He stood and strode over to the parts box, rummaging for a moment before pulling out a replacement. "Easy fix." He returned, clipped the damaged housing off, and then slid the new one into place with practiced hands. A few twists of the screwdriver, and the cable moved smoothly when he gave it a test pull. "There. Good as new."

Nathan watched him work, his gaze tracking the clean motion of the cable. "This is going to be cool when it's finished." He smiled, a little shy. "Thanks for helping me build it."

Recalling his first motorized bike build, Elam couldn't help grinning. "It's going to be more than cool. It's going to be a beast."

Nathan eyed the motor. "How fast will it go?"

"With the load it'll carry? I'd say somewhere around twenty, maybe twenty-five miles an hour. Plenty fast enough to turn some heads."

From across the yard, Reuben's voice rang out. "Just remember the rule. No racing that contraption. You don't need another broken leg."

Nathan rolled his eyes. "*Ach*, parents."

Elam chuckled. "My *mamm* said the same thing." He paused, a sheepish grin tugging at his mouth. "Turns out she wasn't wrong. Except when I wrecked mine, I broke my arm."

Nathan snorted, shaking his head as he studied the frame. "Think we could paint it red? With white trim?"

He nodded. "Definitely. We'll get it looking sharp and smooth in no time."

Just then, the back door creaked open, and Anika stepped out. Her cheeks were flushed from the kitchen heat. "Lunch is almost ready," she called.

"Aw, I'm not ready to stop," Nathan said, tossing down his screwdriver.

"Take a break and you can come back to it later," Reuben said, wheeling himself around on the grassy lawn. His wheelchair hung up, impeding his progress.

"Let me." Elam hurried to help, pushing him gently back toward the house. Using scrap wood, he'd recently built a ramp addition to make it easier for Reuben to get outside. Reuben's father had lent his carpentry skills to ensure the ramp was sturdy and safe.

Anika smiled as they all entered. "Hope you're all hungry."

"Starved," Reuben replied with a laugh, maneuvering his wheelchair toward the kitchen table.

Nathan clambered in, heading down the hall. "Dibs on the washroom," he called, slamming the door behind him.

"Guess that leaves me the kitchen sink," Elam said, pausing to wash his hands. Snagging a towel to dry them, he pulled in a breath. The aromas of simmering stew and freshly baked bread wrapped around him, stirring memories he hadn't allowed himself to feel in years. "It smells amazing."

Anika's cheeks flushed. "*Danke*," she said. "It's *Mamm*'s recipe, just like she used to make it."

"Then I know it'll be great," he said, hanging the towel on its peg. The cozy kitchen, with its gingham curtains and handmade furniture, felt more like home than any place he'd been in years.

And then there was Anika.

Since the night they'd shared that kiss beneath the moonlit sky, nothing more had passed between them. No declarations. No stolen touches. Just a quiet understanding and the kind of ease that grew with time. Before he knew it, he'd somehow stepped into a life he hadn't realized he longed for.

Yet, beneath familiarity, an unwelcome tension twisted in his gut. If he kept hanging around, he couldn't do it halfway. He'd be expected to embrace Amish ways completely. The *Ordnung*. The sacrifices. The surrendering of everything he once knew, including the world outside their community.

He glanced toward Anika as she finished preparing the food, her movements fluid and sure. She was everything good. Gentle, kind and firmly rooted in the Plain life.

He swallowed hard. *Am I strong enough to be worthy of her?*

Anika stirred the stew gently, the warm scents of beef and simmering vegetables rising with the steam. She ladled the thick broth into four bowls, carrying them carefully to the table.

Daed sat in his usual place. Nathan was there, too. And Elam… Somehow, he'd become part of the family.

It felt normal. Almost like the way things used to be.

She went back to the stove and grabbed the rolls, letting herself savor the calm of the moment. After everything they'd been through, days like this were a small miracle. Not perfect. Not quite complete. But better. The family was starting to heal.

Placing the bread in the center of the table, she took her seat. "I made plenty. Dig in."

Daed nodded approvingly. "Looks *gut*." He reached for his napkin but faltered, his face tightening in a sudden grimace. His hand hovered uncertainly in the air, then dropped back to his lap.

Anika sat up straighter. "Are you all right, *Daed*?"

"I'm fine," he said, flexing his fingers, trying to shake off the pain.

"If you say so," she echoed, unsure. *Daed*'s face had lost its usual color, the ruddy warmth replaced by a pallor that made the lines around his mouth seem deeper, more etched.

He wants so badly to be strong again.

And though she prayed for that strength to return, she couldn't shake the fear that he was asking too much of himself too soon.

Forcing a smile, *Daed*'s gaze settled on Elam. "Would you say the blessing?"

Anika blinked in surprise. Her father didn't offer lightly. It meant something.

Elam nodded. "I'd be honored."

"Proceed, please."

Everyone bowed their heads. A hush settled over the table, deep and gentle.

Anika risked a peek toward Elam. Bowing his head, he folded his hands without awkwardness. He'd been coming to church with them for weeks now, sitting quietly among the men, relearning the rhythms of their faith. This moment felt like the next small step.

"Heavenly Father," he began hesitantly, searching for the right words. "We thank You for this meal, and we're grateful for the blessings You've bestowed in bringing us together. Please guide us as we grow in faith and love. In Jesus' name, amen."

"Amen," everyone repeated.

Anika lifted her head and met Elam's gaze. For a heartbeat, the world faded. There was something steady in his eyes that made her breath hitch.

He caught her looking. "What?"

She shook her head. "Nothing." Inside, she quivered. How could just a look from him make her feel like the ground had shifted beneath her?

"That was a fine prayer," *Daed* said, reaching for his spoon. "Let's eat."

Nathan wasted no time. He grabbed a roll, split it open, and slathered it with butter. "About time," he mumbled around a mouthful. "I'm starving." One roll vanished, then another. Like most boys his age, he was a bottomless pit, all gangly limbs and endless appetite. Some days, it felt like no amount of food could keep up with his hunger.

Spreading a napkin across her lap, Anika dipped her spoon into the rich stew. She ate slowly, savoring the familiar taste. But her focus wasn't on the food.

From beneath the fringe of her lashes, she stole another glance at Elam, seated across the table with a quiet ease that both comforted and unsettled her.

He doesn't have to be here.

The notion kept returning like a whisper in the shadows she couldn't ignore. His community service had ended weeks ago. He was free to go back to his old life—whatever was left of it. But he hadn't. He still came, nearly every day. Not as early anymore, now that Nathan was back on his feet and handling most of the outside chores again. But Elam always showed up, often with some part he'd scavenged for Nathan's new bike.

More than that, he'd taken the time to truly know Nathan. In many ways, Elam had stepped into Jason's place, acting like a big brother. And that wasn't a bad thing. Nathan thrived under his attention, learning to build a new bike instead of buying one. He was excited to have something no one else had.

Why? her heart asked before her mind could stop it. *Why is Elam still coming?*

Was it because of her?

And if he was, what then?

She wasn't ready to answer that. The night they'd shared a kiss by the lake, she'd made no promises.

Not with words, anyway. Maybe not even with feelings.

But still, every time Elam arrived, something inside her stirred to the point that she'd begun to imagine a life with him. She could almost picture him walking through the door, wiping his boots at the threshold, greeting her with a smile and…

Her thoughts suddenly stuttered, bringing the daydreams to a halt. Marriage wasn't just love and shared labor. It was prayer. Community. Covenant. And she couldn't carry the burden of believing for both. *Mamm* had taught her that love built on hope alone was like trying to grow corn in stony soil. It might sprout, but it wouldn't last.

A sigh winnowed past her lips. No matter how cozy the visions felt, they always cracked at the edges. Because nothing about them was real.

Not yet. Maybe not ever. Elam had made no steps toward joining the church. No meetings with the bishop. No mention of *gelassenheit* or baptism. No confession of faith.

Appetite vanishing, Anika quietly set her spoon aside. How could she truly open her heart to someone who hadn't yet opened his to *Gott*?

The truth was clear. She simply couldn't.

Across the table, *Daed*'s face drained of color. His hand trembled, fingers twitching weakly, unresponsive to his own will. "I can't feel my fingers."

"*Daed*?" Anika jumped up, heart pounding.

"What's wrong?" Nathan cried in alarm.

Wincing again, *Daed* swallowed hard. "I think I need to go to the hospital." As he spoke, fear flickered in his eyes.

Panic surged through Anika, freezing her in place. The kitchen blurred and swayed, the walls closing in as dread wrapped icy fingers around her. Memories of the accident crashed over her, suffocating and raw. She grasped the edge of the table, desperate to steady herself, but it was no use. Fear pressed hard, stealing her breath.

And then calm emerged through the chaos.

Elam was already on his feet. "Nathan, get the buggy!" he ordered, taking control. "We need to go. Now. It'll be faster to get him to the hospital ourselves."

"*Ja*, I will!" Nathan turned fast and ran hard. The slam of the screen door echoed behind him.

After that, everything became a blur.

Later, Anika couldn't remember how they got *Daed* into the buggy or how Elam managed to get them into town. The world felt distant and muffled, like she was moving through water. Sounds came in fragments: *Daed*'s moans of pain, the steady clip of the horse's hooves, Nathan calling out directions. Elam's voice grounded her now and then, firm and steady, but even that faded under the crush of her fear.

Somehow, they made it to the emergency room, where *Daed* was immediately whisked away for examination.

Now, hours later, they waited in a narrow hallway at the small hospital.

Anika sat hunched in a stiff plastic chair, fingers knotted in her lap. Elam paced a few feet away, arms folded tight across his chest. Nathan sat with his hands clasped between his knees, staring at the speckled tile floor.

At last, a doctor stepped through the doors, clipboard in hand. "I'm looking for the family of Reuben Glick."

Anika stood on trembling legs. It was just like before. The waiting. The not knowing. "That's us."

"How is *Daed*?" Nathan asked before she could.

The physician consulted his notes. "Mr. Glick has severe shoulder tendinitis with a partial rotator cuff tear and signs of nerve irritation. We confirmed it with imaging."

"Will he be all right?" Elam asked.

"With the right care, yes," the doctor replied in a calm, clinical tone. "But this won't heal on its own. He's in significant pain, and his range of motion is already restricted." He glanced again at his clipboard. "I understand he's been trying to exercise independently?"

"He has," Elam said. "He's been working hard to build upper-body strength."

"I admire the initiative," the doctor said, "but without professional guidance, that kind of effort can do more harm than good. In his case, it likely worsened the inflammation."

Anika felt her heart drop. "What does that mean?"

"He needs supervised physical therapy," the doctor continued. "Targeted exercises, two to three times a week. Without it, he risks a full rotator cuff tear or permanent nerve damage. Surgery would then become much more likely."

"How soon should therapy start?" Nathan asked.

"As soon as possible. We'll provide a referral and set up a treatment plan with a licensed therapist. Delays could severely impact his long-term mobility."

Anika swallowed, dread coiling tight. Therapy meant appointments. It meant travel. But more than anything, it meant money. And that was something they didn't have. Every precious dollar was already spoken for.

"We've given him an anti-inflammatory injection and prescribed oral pain medication to manage his discomfort at home," the doctor said. "He's stable and can be discharged tonight, but he'll need help getting around until the pain subsides."

"Thank you," Elam said.

As the doctor turned and walked away, Anika's knees buckled. A wave of helplessness washed over her, and she sank back into the chair. "This isn't *gut* news."

"There's no way we can do this," Nathan added, giving voice to the stark truth. "If we could afford it, *Daed* would have had the help a long time ago."

Elam stepped up, looking between them both. "Don't worry," he said, speaking in a firm tone. "Everything will be covered."

Startled by the certainty in his tone, Anika glanced up. "How?"

"I said don't worry." Jaw set, Elam's eyes were fierce with determination. "Reuben will get the therapy he needs. I'll see to it."

Anika blinked, stunned. Elam was out of work and had been for months.

How could he possibly take care of something like this?

Chapter Fifteen

The afternoon sun hung low in the sky, casting a glow over the modest yard.

Elam leaned against the split-rail fence, his arms crossed, watching his brother work in the garden. A few feet away, Abram knelt, a straw hat shading his face as he tied tomato vines to stakes with practiced ease. The work seemed effortless for him, a task he was comfortable with.

"I wondered if you'd be coming around again."

Scuffing the ground with his boot, Elam sent a clump of dirt flying. "Didn't know if I'd be welcome."

"You've always been welcome," Abram replied, not looking up. "No one's stopped you but you."

Elam's mouth quirked up. Nothing about his older brother had changed. Not his manner, nor the quiet way he pointed out the facts. "I guess you're right. I did drift off."

"Heard you might be drifting back," Abram continued conversationally. "Word around is you're still going to church."

"I have." He'd taken to attending the biweekly services, sitting near the back at first, then gradually finding his place among the familiar faces. As he cycled through various hosts and locations in the district, folks he hadn't spoken to in years were starting to greet him with cautious warmth.

Abram pulled a stubborn weed, tossing it aside. "Happy to hear it. I think it's *gut* for you."

"I'm trying," he admitted. "I don't know if I understand everything, but I am listening."

Abram glanced up. "What don't you understand?"

"All of it," he admitted, threading his fingers together. "About what it means to have such a deep belief. To trust in something you can't see."

"That's understandable. A lot of folks struggle with it."

"I'm trying to get it," Elam said, spreading his hands for emphasis. "And I'm open to considering someone's there." He lifted his eyes to the sky, watching a hawk circle overhead. "Listening."

Abram paused, studying him. "But?"

Elam let out a slow breath. "I haven't heard God speak. Not in the way everyone talks about. And, um, I guess I keep wondering if that means I'm not listening right. Or if maybe He just doesn't talk to people like me."

Abram straightened, resting his hands on his knees. "He does talk to people like you," he said. "And like me. Like all of us. But not always in ways we expect."

"Then why can't I hear Him?"

"Sometimes we have to live through the silence before we can recognize the voice. We want answers right away, but the Lord doesn't work on our timetable. He speaks when the time is right. When He knows we're ready to listen, not just with our ears, but with our hearts."

Elam looked down, his thumb rubbing over a scar on his knuckle. "What if I never get there? What if I've messed up too much?"

"You're already on the path. You're asking the right questions. You're wrestling with the truth, and that's more honest than pretending to have all the answers."

"Is it?"

"Even then. Especially then."

"You think there's hope for me?"

Abram nodded. “When the Lord is ready, He’ll speak. And when He does, you’ll know it.”

“I’d like Him to,” Elam said, the words sticking. “I’ve got some questions.”

“Oh?” Abram tilted his head. “What’s on your mind?”

Elam stared at the ground. “I don’t know if I should say.”

Abram chuckled. “I’m not the Lord, but I’ve got two ears and a bit of wisdom. Maybe I can help.”

“It’s a girl,” he blurted. “I’ve got feelings for her. Strong ones. And I don’t know what to do with them.”

A faint smile tugged at his brother’s mouth. “Would the girl you’re speaking about be Anika Glick?”

Elam’s gaze flicked up, surprised. “How’d you know?”

“*Ach*, it’s a small town and gossip has gone around.”

Elam gave a weak laugh, then turned serious. “We’re not courting or anything,” he hastened to explain. “But we’ve been spending time together. More than I expected. And I know people have started to notice.” He exhaled, a mix of frustration and longing. “I didn’t go looking for this. I thought I’d serve my time, fix what I broke and move on after my community service ended.”

Abram raised a brow. “But that’s not how it’s going, is it?”

Elam hesitated, then spread his hands in a gesture of helpless honesty. “I don’t know how to walk away. I like Anika. A lot. And not just because she’s pretty. It’s the way she keeps going even when everything’s falling apart. Being around her makes me want to help, you know. Take care of her…”

“Does she know how you feel?”

“Kind of,” he admitted. He’d dated a few girls before, but it was casual, nothing lasting. This felt different. Serious. And he wasn’t sure what to do with that. “I said a few things…and we’ve kissed. But nothing since then.”

“Why not?”

"Because I'm scared. Scared of what it could mean. For her, for me. For everything."

A stern look settled over Abram's face as he spoke. "You may think you're being careful, but you can't straddle the fence."

He blinked. "What do you mean?"

"I mean, Anika Glick doesn't need someone playing with her emotions. You're either serious about her or you're not. If you want to be in her life, then be in it. All the way."

"I'm not playing games," Elam countered. "I'd never do that to her."

"I believe you," Abram replied. "But that doesn't change what's true. You've got one foot in the *Englisch* world and the other still touching ours. You can't keep jumping between the two. It's not fair to her. Anika's already been through enough. She deserves someone sure. Someone who's all in."

"I don't want to lose her." Elam hesitated, fists curling with quiet desperation. "But I don't know if I can go back to Amish."

"What trips you up isn't being Amish," Abram pointed out. "It's the *Ordnung*. Always has been. You want to live on your terms."

Elam looked away. His brother had struck a nerve. "Why does everything about being Plain have to come with so many rules?"

Abram tipped back his straw hat and looked at him over the rim of his glasses. "The *Ordnung* is more than a list of rules. It's the foundation of our community. It keeps us humble and focused on the path *Gott* set before us."

"But sometimes it feels like we're just following orders. Where's the freedom in that?"

"Freedom?" Abram's brow lifted. "Real freedom isn't doing whatever you want. It's knowing that your choices honor *Gott* and bring peace to others. The *Ordnung* doesn't chain us—it protects us. The outside world might glitter, but it's full of snares that'll pull a man away from grace."

"That sounds like exactly what a minister would say."

"Maybe it is," Abram admitted. "But I'm not speaking as a minister. I'm speaking as your blood kin. I want you to have a *gut* life. To marry and have *kinder.* To know the joy of building something that lasts. But you can't do that with one foot out the door."

"Let's not talk about it," he said, feeling the truth press hard. He couldn't keep drifting in uncertainty, but where exactly he belonged still eluded him. "That's not why I came."

"Then why are you here?"

Elam hesitated. "Do you have any work at the market?" Founded by his grandfather, the place had grown into a thriving business under Abram's management, offering produce, baked goods, and handmade crafts from the Plain community.

Surprise flickered across his brother's face. "You're asking for a job?"

"Yeah."

"I could use help with stocking shelves and packing orders," Abram said. "It's not your usual kind of work, but the pay's decent. Or, if you're interested, Rolf's looking for help at the retreat."

Elam grimaced. He'd had more than his fill of farmwork. "I'll take the market job," he said. "Do you still send a van for workers? I'll need a ride back and forth."

Abram smiled. "If you lived closer, you could ride with me."

"Yeah, but I don't."

"You could consider taking over Gran'pa's *haus,*" Abram continued. "It's sitting empty since he passed."

He snorted, shaking his head. "That old place?" he scoffed. "It's got no electricity, no propane and only cold running water."

"If you sold your garage, you'd have enough to rebuild your savings and start fresh here."

Elam looked around. The Mueller family property sat on the edge of Humble, surrounded by lush hills, hardwood trees and a pond perfect for fishing. Though it had originally been purchased by his *grossdaadi* Amos, each family member had inherited a parcel to build on. Elam had sold his share to buy the property in town, a move that once felt like the right step toward independence. Big mistake. His eldest brother, Rolf, had generously purchased the adjoining acreage and lovingly shaped it into the Humble Hearth Rural Retreat, a peaceful haven for guests hoping to experience a taste of Amish life.

Now, something pinched in his chest. He'd traded the permanence of home and family for a run-down garage in town.

I should have figured out a way to make it work.

But that was the thing about regret. Hindsight was always sharp, clear—and usually came too late to be of any use.

Still, he stood there, caught in the gravity of his own indecision. The truth pressed, but the words wouldn't come. Swallowing a stone would be easier than admitting he'd made a mistake.

Caught in the tug-of-war with himself, he sighed. "I'm not sure I'm ready to take that step."

"You mean come back to the family?" Abram said, giving him a pointed look over the edge of his glasses.

He let out a slow sigh. "Yeah… That."

"The longer you sit on the fence, the more likely you are to fall and lose everything on both sides," Abram countered, speaking the truth.

The remark hit hard.

Thoughts churning, Elam felt his insides tighten. Could he return to the Amish? Step back into that world as if nothing had changed? Part of him wanted to believe it was possible. That love and faith were enough.

But fear gnawed harder, whispering that it wouldn't be easy. To be with Anika, he'd have to do more than just go back. He'd have to recommit. To the faith. To the *Ordnung*. To a life stripped of *Englisch* ways.

Is this where I'm meant to be?

It was a question only he could answer. And he'd have to. Soon.

Because if he couldn't, he'd have to walk away.

Anika pushed open the bedroom door with her shoulder, the hinges creaking softly. The midday sun filtered through the thin lace curtain, casting pale patterns over the neatly made bed and the man resting atop it. Her father reclined against a mound of pillows, his right arm propped carefully on a cushion to avoid aggravating his injured shoulder. His Bible lay closed on his lap, but he wasn't reading. His gaze was on the window, distant and heavy.

"Daed?"

He turned his head toward her, managing a tired smile. "You don't have to check on me every hour."

She walked to his bedside. "I'm about to start lunch. Is there anything you're in the mood for today?"

Daed gave a soft huff, but the sadness in his eyes lingered. "Whatever you make is fine. I'm not very hungry."

Anika's gaze swept over his gaunt frame. Since coming home from the hospital a few days ago, her father had barely touched his food. He spent most of his time confined to his room, lying in bed or quietly reading his Bible. The doctors had urged rest until therapy could begin, but he showed no interest in either. It wasn't just physical exhaustion; it was something heavier. A slow, quiet retreat from life. And it scared her.

"You have to eat, *Daed*."

He let out a weary sigh. "What for?"

"You need your strength."

"So I can sit in that wheelchair some more?" Shaking his head, her father frowned. "I'm tired of being tied to it."

"You won't be forever," she replied, trying to offer hope.

"Once you start your appointments, the doctors will help you. Please, give them a chance."

"We don't have the money—" *Daed* began.

Anika cut him off. "You're not to think about that."

Daed narrowed his eyes. "Don't tell me *Poppi*'s planning to sell off some land."

She hesitated, remembering how her grandfather had spoken of it in the dark days after the accident. But *Daed* had been adamant. The property stayed with the family. It was more than soil and fences. It was history. Legacy. A place to build and belong.

"*Nein*," she said, shaking her head. "That hasn't changed."

"Then how?" he demanded, frustration sharpening his voice. "How are we supposed to afford this?"

Anika reached for his hand, her voice steady. "Because we follow *Gott*, and He will always make a way," she said, offering a smile. "Isn't that what you always told me?"

Daed's gaze drifted to the worn Bible resting in his lap. "You're right. I need to believe that things will work out."

She smiled. "Just trust the Lord that everything's going to be all right."

Daed nodded, a quiet peace easing the creases around his mouth. "*Danke* for the reminder," he said, his fingers brushing the delicate pages of the Bible. "In the book of John, it says, 'Blessed are they that have not seen, and yet have believed.' I reckon it's time I doubt less and pray more."

Relief softened the tightness in Anika's chest. They were all carrying heavy loads, but she knew keeping close to *Gottes Wort* would help see them through.

"I'll get started on lunch," she said. "How does baked chicken with mashed potatoes sound?"

"I could eat," *Daed* agreed, thankfully.

Leaving him to his reading, she stepped into the kitchen, her footsteps soft against the worn wooden floor. The house felt unusually still, too silent, as if it were holding its breath.

She reached for the battery-powered radio and switched it on, instinctively skipping past the familiar pop or country standards she usually favored. Instead, her fingers stopped on a gospel station. Since returning to church and immersing herself in Bible study, she longed for a deeper connection, a quiet assurance that the Lord was nearby.

As the music filled the kitchen, she gathered the ingredients, setting them on the counter. Her gaze drifted toward the window, where the yard lay still beneath the soft, golden glow of late-morning sunlight.

Despite the music's soothing presence, a restless unease settled over her. Days had slipped by since she'd last seen Elam.

Why hasn't he come back?

The question looped through her mind, steady and unrelenting. He'd told her he wasn't the kind to cut and run. But boys said all sorts of things when they were trying to prove themselves. Maybe he'd reached his limit. Her family had problems, enough to make anyone think twice. Maybe *Daed*'s trip to the hospital had been too much. And now, with his community service over, he had no reason to stay. No obligation to them. Or to her.

Her jaw clenched as she seasoned the chicken before laying it in a pan for baking. She didn't think Elam would disappear like that. But still, he was free to do whatever he pleased.

The back door creaked open, followed by the thud of boots on the threshold. Anika turned to see Nathan entering, hot and dusty from the morning's chores.

"Think most everything's done," he said, pulling off his hat and hanging it on the peg.

"You didn't have to do all that alone," Anika said, sliding the pan into the oven. "I was going to help after lunch."

He shrugged. "A man's got to take care of his place."

Anika paused, watching him wipe the sweat from his brow. He was right. Now that Jason was gone, Nathan was the eldest *sohn.* The farm would pass to him one day, just as it should. As a woman, her path was different. She was expected to marry, move to her *ehemann*'s home and start fresh somewhere else.

Spending time with Elam, she'd allowed herself to spin a few fanciful daydreams, believing he would be the one she'd someday start a new life with. But since he'd been away, she wondered if she'd misread his intentions. Perhaps the days they'd shared hadn't meant as much to him as they had to her. She was probably foolish for thinking he was sincere when he said he wanted to continue being a part of their lives.

"You're doing a *gut* job, Nathan," she said, shoving the thoughts aside. Dwelling on it wouldn't change anything. All it would do is make her feel worse.

"I've been thinking," he said, heading to the sink to wash his hands. "Once the bike's finished, I'm going to look for a job in town."

"A job?" she echoed. "Where?"

"Maybe at the feed store. Or at the pharmacy, doing deliveries. We need the money, and I intend to pull my weight."

Tears pricked her eyes. She nodded, overwhelmed by her younger brother. Nathan might be a handful, but when it mattered most, he showed up. Willing. Steady. Stronger than he let on. At an age when Amish boys were expected to commit to apprenticeships or take up the family trade, his declaration marked his first real step into manhood.

"You already do," she whispered.

Before he could answer, a knock sounded at the front door.

"Now, who could that be?" she wondered aloud, wiping her hands on a clean rag. As far as she knew, they weren't expecting company today. Smoothing her apron, she hurried to open the door.

Elam stood there, his backpack slung over one shoulder. "Hey."

Relief blossomed. "Hey," she replied. "Come on in." Stepping aside, she motioned toward the kitchen. "You're just in time to join us for lunch."

Trailing in her wake, Elam smiled. "Sounds good."

Nathan grinned from where he stood. "Where've you been, dude?"

"Working," Elam said, setting his carryall down by the door. "I got a job."

"Where?" Nathan asked eagerly.

"At my family's market," Elam replied. "Loading stock, cleaning up, helping with deliveries, whatever needs doing." He gave a small shrug. "I'm sorry that I haven't been around. Getting used to the schedule's been a little hectic."

"That's not the sort of work I'd expect you'd want to do," Anika said, returning to her cooking.

"It'll do until I can get my own business off the ground," Elam explained. "What matters is the pay's fair, and I can help with Reuben's therapy."

A hush fell over the kitchen.

Nathan stared, speechless.

Unsure she'd heard right, Anika blinked. "You what?"

Elam looked between her and Nathan, confusion flickering in his eyes. "I said I would," he replied. "And I meant it."

He'd made the offer, but she hadn't truly expected him to follow through.

"That's generous of you," she said. "But it's not your burden to carry."

"Yeah, it is," he insisted. "I don't know what the future looks like, but I'm going to be part of whatever comes next—" his gaze held hers, steady and sincere "—if you'll all let me."

Breath catching, Anika pressed a trembling hand to her chest. Her heart thudded against her palm. She'd prayed so hard for *Daed*'s therapy to come through. And now this unexpected answer. Once again, *Gott* had shown His mighty power, sweeping away every obstacle.

"You mean that?" she asked, trembling.

"Yeah," he said, and reached for her hand. The warmth of his touch steadied her. "I'm in for the long haul."

Nathan's grin widened. "Glad you're sticking around."

Words failed her, but none were needed. His kindness felt too big, too sudden. Now, she saw it for what it truly was.

Elam wasn't just offering help.

He was choosing to stay.

A single tear trekked down her cheek, not born of grief, but something softer. Relief. Peace spread inside her, filling the hollow spaces that had ached for so long. The future no longer loomed with shadows. A healing light had broken through the darkness enveloping their lives.

Dependable, steady and sure, Elam had made his intentions clear.

And she wouldn't want it any other way.

Chapter Sixteen

The wheelchair lift groaned again, then gave a pitiful buzz and sagged even lower. It just wouldn't work. At all.

Elam grunted, pushing himself out from under the church van, wrench still in hand and sweat clinging to his brow.

"Come on," he muttered, tossing the tool onto the floor. "You're not even trying."

The mechanism had been a mess from the start. By the look of things, it was installed by someone who didn't know what they were doing: bad wiring, mismatched bolts and all. It had taken hours to untangle the mess. He'd replaced the relay switch, tested the power line and rewired the terminals. Still, no movement. Just a wheeze and a whine.

He leaned back on his heels and ran a hand through his damp hair, jaw tightening. This van had potential once it was fixed. The frame was solid, the engine decent. The wheelchair lift was the biggest problem. However, with enough time and tinkering, even that would come around. The van wasn't perfect, but it had a purpose. Once it was running, it would serve the disabled members of the church. Plenty of volunteer drivers were already lined up, mostly unbaptized young men willing to do their part. It stung Elam that he couldn't be one of them. Losing his license still felt like a punch to the gut every time he thought about it.

But it wasn't forever.

He picked up the wrench again and tightened the mounting bolts on the motor, hands moving out of habit. Again, the motor buzzed when powered, but the platform didn't rise.

He huffed. Likely a short in the control panel or a failed solenoid.

Still, it was nothing he couldn't fix. He'd made worse things run.

Needing a break, he pushed away from the van. Sweat soaked the collar of his T-shirt. His muscles ached, and his back twinged from too much time contorted beneath the vehicle.

Walking over to the cooler, he flipped the lid and reached into its icy depths. His fingers found a cold can, slick with condensation. He cracked it open and took a long sip, letting the chill fizz wash the dryness from his throat. The old oscillating fan in the corner hummed as it swept a slow, lazy arc across the shop. The garage had no air-conditioning, part of the reason he'd gotten the property at a reduced price. The fan didn't help much, but it was better than nothing.

Elam dropped onto the bench, resting the cold can against the side of his neck. He stretched out his legs, letting the worn soles of his boots scrape against the concrete floor, and leaned his head back against the wall.

Silence settled around him.

A long while had passed since he'd spent any time in the garage. Lately, it had just become a place to sleep.

His gaze drifted toward the ceiling. Above the garage sat a small efficiency apartment. For a bachelor, it worked. All he needed was a place to crash after long hours at work. Nothing more. It wasn't the kind of place to bring a girlfriend. And it sure wasn't any kind of place to start a life with a wife.

Elam winced. *How're you going to get married if you haven't got a proper home?*

The notion had buzzed through his mind since Anika came into his life. Quiet at first, it grew louder with every passing day they spent together. He thought about her more than he cared to admit.

And he couldn't shake the idea that, someday, he'd marry her.

"Get it out of your head," he muttered. But he couldn't. Something he hadn't wanted in the *Englisch* world looked enticing when viewed from the Amish side.

He took another drink from his soda, turning the notion over in his mind. Moving into his grandfather's old house would mean more than a change of address. It meant letting go of the life he'd built, the freedom, the noise, the identity he'd once fought so hard to carve out. Now that his community service was over, he could go back to living as he pleased. He could walk away from the Glicks. From the church. From the simplicity. He could pick up where he left off, doing what he wanted, when he wanted.

But the truth didn't sit that cleanly. It hadn't been simple for a long time. Something had taken root and somehow, he'd gotten attached. To Reuben. To Nathan. Most of all to Anika.

Without meaning to, he'd become part of their lives. The farm had drawn him in with its honest work and steady pace. He liked tending the animals, making repairs and hanging out on the back porch after supper. He liked sitting at a table, eating meals prepared with a loving touch. He didn't even mind the long church services, sitting shoulder to shoulder with others who shared his doubts, his fears, his longing for a true connection with something more. There was peace in that life, a kind he hadn't known he was missing.

Shaking his head, he sighed. Abram had warned him that straddling the fence between two different worlds wouldn't work much longer. He had to pick a side and stick to it. If he was serious about staying and pursuing a relationship with Anika, it was time to start thinking that way.

Without quite meaning to, his eyes drifted toward the Dodge. Still uncovered, the car sat beneath the high windows, half in shadow, half in light. Every curve and line seemed to shimmer with raw, untamed power.

Unlike the van, it was perfect. He'd finished the restoration only weeks before everything fell apart. After all the time and money he'd invested, it should've been a triumph.

Now it just sat there, gathering silence.

Narrowing his eyes, Elam studied the vintage car. Selling it would solve a lot of problems. A classic like that could bring in a lot of money. Six figures, easy—if he found the right buyer. That kind of cash would easily cover the bills for Reuben's physical therapy. It would also be enough to launch a small business. A future, built from the ground up.

He should've felt pride when he looked at it. Satisfaction for the hours he'd poured into the restoration.

Instead, all he felt was a hollow sense of loss.

He leaned forward, the can of soda sweating in his grip. From everything he'd learned in church, surrendering one's will to a higher power was the foundation of true faith. When a man hit a crossroads, when his heart was tangled and uncertain, he wasn't supposed to act on impulse. He was supposed to pray.

"Lord," he whispered, voice nearly lost beneath the hum of the fan, "I'm waiting for You to give me some answers about my thoughts. I'm trying to walk the path You want, but I don't know if I'm even on it."

Silence.

Once again, no answer.

Sighing, Elam crushed the empty can and tossed it in a nearby trash can. "Guess that's that." He stood, torn between the man he'd been and the one he was trying to become.

The low growl of an engine suddenly rolled up the gravel drive leading to the garage. Outside, tires crunched to a stop.

Frowning, Elam walked to the open bay door. He wasn't expecting anyone.

An El Camino idled just outside. The engine shut off, and a familiar figure stepped out.

Elam stiffened. He hadn't seen Chris Weaver since the night everything went sideways—and they both ended up in the back of a squad car. Chris hadn't changed much. Same cocky strut, denim jacket and worn jeans, hair slicked back like he was still starring in his own outlaw movie. Sunglasses perched on his forehead completed the look, like he couldn't decide if he was too cool or just didn't care.

"Dude," he said, lifting a hand in greeting. "Been looking for you."

Elam crossed his arms. He'd heard Chris was out, but he hadn't gone looking. He didn't need that kind of trouble knocking on his door. Not now. Not after everything. The fact that Chris was still behind the wheel didn't surprise him. His old friend always had a way of skating past consequences like the laws weren't made for him.

"I'm not hard to find."

"Yeah, you are," Chris said. "Been trying to catch up with you since they let me out of the clink a few weeks ago. Word around is you're back to hanging with the plow-pulling puritans."

He shrugged, letting the slur go by. "Yeah, so what? In case you forgot, I'm Amish."

Chris snorted. "Oh, come on. That isn't you, by a long shot." He grinned. "Those people think electricity is wicked and a good time is a sin."

"Maybe I've changed."

"Relax." Chris raised his hands. "Just making conversation."

"Then say what you got to and go," he replied. "I'm busy."

Grinning, Chris tilted his head. "Too busy for a race?"

Elam's stomach flipped. He gave Chris a wary look. "What kind?"

"There's a race Saturday night. Back lane between Ontario and La Farge, near that old logging trail. Real straight. Real quiet."

"Who's putting it together?"

"A couple of guys out of Westby. They've done it before, low-key. Nine cars signed on, just need one more."

"What's the payout?"

"Winner takes twenty-five. Rest goes to the pot—flagger, spotters and all that." Chris glanced over his shoulder, then dropped his voice. "Sheriff in Vernon County knows it's happening. His kid's racing."

Elam gave a dry snort. "The one with the LeMans?"

"Yep."

"He won't win."

Chris grinned. "Exactly. Sheriff's deal is he'll look the other way 'cos he thinks his boy has a chance."

"What's the buy-in?"

"Three grand."

Elam let out a low whistle. His paycheck barely scratched the surface. Even with the meager amount he had left in savings, he'd still come up short. "Can't swing it."

Chris leaned in. "You'd be a fool to pass this up."

"I don't have the money," he repeated, irritation seeping through. "You racing the El Camino?"

"Wouldn't miss it." Chris swaggered over, running a hand over the Challenger's gleaming hood. "How can you let this baby sit out?"

Elam squared his shoulders. "Like I said, don't have the cash."

Chris's eyes gleamed. "What if I cover your buy-in? You win, you pay me back five."

The offer hit like a shot of adrenaline.

Elam straightened. Chris Weaver's Chevrolet was fast, no

question. But his Dodge Challenger with its 426-cubic-inch V8 was a speed demon. There was no doubt in his mind that it could take this. And twenty grand? That could change everything.

Just do it.

Win the race. Then sell the car, no regrets. Just the satisfaction of knowing the restoration was worth it. And the money? It could give him and Anika the fresh start they both deserved.

It was all so very tempting.

Then he shook his head. Hadn't he learned the difference between recklessness and responsibility?

"You know I lost my license." A weak excuse, but it was all he had.

"Same," Chris said, confirming what Elam already knew. "No one cares about that but the law. What matters is if you've got the nerve to drive and the skill to win."

Licking dry lips, Elam walked over to his pride and joy. The vehicle's metallic-blue shade gleamed in the stretch of sunlight filtering through the open bay, shimmering like temptation made flesh.

"What if I lose?"

"Then I'm out the buy-in," Chris said with a grin. "But you won't. I know this car's specs just as well as you do. It's the fastest thing on wheels in this dead-end town. It'll smoke the competition."

Elam wavered. He didn't need to close his eyes to imagine the roar of the engine, the shift of gears, the surge of power when he pressed the accelerator.

Do it, the devious voice whispered again.

Take the car out on his terms. Let it prove itself. Let *him* prove himself. Then he'd have closure and a clean slate to start over as an Amish man.

His jaw tightened. He'd prayed for direction. Was this the answer?

Swallowing doubt, he pivoted back to Chris. "I'm in."

* * *

Anika set the last plate in the drying rack and reached for a towel, drying her hands with slow, weary motions. The kitchen had gone still, the earlier clatter of dishes and supper conversation fading into the hush of evening. Heated by the old cookstove, the air hung thick around her, wrapping her in a stifling embrace.

"I don't think I can take much more of this temperature," she murmured, swaying slightly as a wave of dizziness rolled over her.

Beside her, Elam finished rinsing the dishpan and set it aside with a clunk. "It's like standing in an oven," he said, dragging a hand across his damp forehead. "I don't know how you bear it."

Anika let out a weary laugh. The battery-powered fans barely offered any relief. "It's always like this in the summer."

He backed away from the sink, fluttering his T-shirt to stir a bit of breeze. "I could use a little air," he said, nodding toward the back door. "Come with me?"

Flushed, she nodded. "That does sound nice."

They stepped out into the fading day, the screen door creaking shut behind them. The scent of peonies drifted in the air, mingling with grass and the faint, musky odor of the livestock. Crickets had already begun their evening song, and fireflies winked lazily in the hedgerows.

Elam led her to the swing under the maple tree, and they sat side by side. The bench creaked gently as it rocked beneath them, the rhythm soothing after a long day.

Anika folded her hands in her lap, grateful for the cool breeze. Now that the long day of chores was behind her, it felt good to get off her feet. Enjoying the quiet evening, *Daed* had settled in with his book. Nathan had gone out to check on the livestock and bed down the animals for the night.

Elam had been gone for a few days, but she'd come to expect that. Between long hours at the market and working on the church van, his time was pulled in too many directions. Still, she couldn't help but miss him when he wasn't around.

"I'm glad you were able to come by tonight," she said, opening the conversation.

He grinned. "Well, I didn't want to keep the news to myself."

"I can't believe the van's already done," she said, shaking her head at the memory of his announcement.

"Got the work done as fast as I could," he confirmed. "It's ready to roll, and I'll be turning it over to Bishop Graber tomorrow."

Anika remembered the way her father's face had lit up when he heard the news. "*Daed*'s so excited. He'll finally be able to get around with some dignity." She turned to him, sincerity in her voice. "*Danke* for giving that back to him."

"Happy to do it." Shaking his head, he added. "It had its issues, but I think I got them all. That lift just didn't want to work."

"But you figured it out."

"Yeah," he said, shrugging. "I did."

"Nathan has been working on his bike," she continued. "Says once the motor's on, he can get to town faster. He's talking about looking for a job, too, so this will help him get around."

Elam grinned. "The kid's got drive. And he's a fast learner. That's half the battle."

"I haven't seen him this happy in a long time. *Danke* for helping him." Throat squeezing with emotion, she added, "For helping all of us."

He shook his head. "I didn't do anything special."

"You did," she insisted. "You've given all hope again."

Shrugging, Elam kicked at the grass with one boot. "I just wanted to help."

They continued to swing gently, the evening deepening around them. Purple shadows pooled at the base of the trees.

"I've been thinking," he said after a pause. "About what's coming next. About the future."

She glanced at him. "You are?"

"Yeah. I didn't expect things to turn around so quickly, but they are. I've got a way to get ahead. Faster than I thought."

Curiosity stirred. "Oh?"

He hesitated, then sat forward, hands braced on his knees. "There's a race tomorrow night, out near La Farge. It's big. Well organized. And there's a huge payout."

Anika blinked. "A race?"

He nodded. "I'm going to enter and win."

Her stomach dropped. "I thought the judge took your license."

"He did, but I'll be fine. The sheriff knows about it. He's looking the other way because his kid's got a car in the race."

"That doesn't mean it's right."

"I know it's risky," he admitted, "but it's one race. One and done. If I win, I can cover Reuben's therapy. Maybe more. And…we'd be one step closer to marrying."

She froze. "To what?"

"To marrying," he repeated, looking at her with quiet certainty.

Anika pulled back. "I can't marry you.".

"Why not?"

"You're not Amish," she blurted.

"I intend to be."

She shook her head, frustration rising. "Intending isn't enough," she said, trying to keep her voice steady. "Until you formally rejoin the church, it's just talk."

"I plan to," he countered. "After the race. After I've done what I need to do. I'll sell the Dodge. My garage, too. I want a clean slate, for us. I can fix up my grandfather's old house. It needs work, but it's something to start with."

Pulse racing, Anika stared at him. "You've made all these plans, but without me. You never asked what I wanted."

"I thought it was pretty obvious," he said. "I care about you. And you care about me. It's not just in my head, is it?"

"I've thought about it," she admitted. "You're a *gut* man. And you've done so much for my family. But you're putting the cart before the horse. Literally."

He raked a hand through his hair, frustration flaring. "I'm just trying to build something—for us."

"Is that so?" she demanded, skeptically.

"Yeah. That's so."

"How?"

"I just told you. I'm doing this for our future." Irritation twisted his mouth. "It's just one race. Let me have this. One. Last. Thing."

"So you can prove what?" she countered. "That you're still the cool guy you used to be?"

"It's a lot more than that."

"Like what?"

"Like everything," he flung back, voice roughening. "I just know I have to do this."

She gave him a hard look. "If you do, we're finished."

Elam's hands opened in a helpless, pleading gesture. "Don't say that."

"I mean it," she said, firmer now. "Get behind that wheel, and that's it. I'll never speak to you again."

He stood suddenly, the swing lurching. "I've bent over backward to help you and your family. I did everything I could. And now you're throwing it back in my face?"

Anika bristled. How dare he make this about all he'd done, as if her family had begged for his help, as if they owed him anything at all.

"If you're here because you felt sorry for us, we don't need your pity." Hands clenching with anger, her nails dug into her palms. "Or your money."

He flinched. "That's not what I meant."

"Then what did you mean?"

"I don't know." Elam let out a breath, arms thrown wide. "I've never felt like this before. It scares me. But I know I want something real between us."

"I want that, too," she said, rising to join him. "But I can't stand by and watch you throw away everything you've worked so hard to rebuild. Not for this. Not for some illegal race."

"I can do it," he insisted. "I can win the money."

"I believe you," she said and put a hand on his arm. "But I'm asking you not to."

Disappointment flickered in his gaze. "I thought you'd be happy."

"Not when you're putting yourself at risk," she said. "What if something happened?" She didn't want to remind him, but the last time he'd raced, Nathan had gotten hurt. Surely the memory haunted him as much as it did her.

"Nothing's going to happen." He dragged a hand through his hair, jaw clenched. "If that's how little confidence you have, maybe we don't have a future."

Anika flinched but steadied herself. "Don't twist my words," she said, striving to match his frustration with quiet resolve. "I'm asking you to think about the future, the one you say you want." Her fingers curled tighter around his arm, anchoring him. "If you're still drawn to things like this, then Plain life won't make you happy. You'd have to follow the *Ordnung*. And I don't believe you can."

Elam's expression shuttered, turning distant. "You're right," he admitted, stepping away. "I'm tired of pretending. I want my old life back."

His confession hit like a slap.

"Then go," she flung, before she could stop herself. "If the *Englisch* world is what you want, then you don't belong here."

"Fine. I'm going." Turning on his heel, Elam stormed out the back gate, pulling his phone from his pocket. Calling a friend for a ride, no doubt.

Anika stared after him. The fireflies flickered around her like silent witnesses to the wreckage.

Just like that, everything had unraveled.

Again.

Chapter Seventeen

Elam sat stiffly in the passenger seat of the Dodge. Arms folded tight across his chest, his gaze was fixed on the dark ribbon of road ahead. His knee bounced restlessly, heel thudding against the floorboard in a rapid rhythm. The smells of motor oil and leather filled the cabin, comforting and suffocating all at once. Outside, the last hints of twilight clung to the sky, but full dark was coming fast, stretching long shadows across the two-lane highway.

Restless, he sighed for the third time in as many minutes. The sun had sunk beneath the hills an hour ago, painting the western sky in streaks of orange and gold that had long since faded to dusky blue. The headlights cast twin beams onto the blacktop, stretching out into the dark like a tunnel. Soon, they'd arrive at their destination and the event would begin.

Ten cars. Ten drivers. One winner.

He'd been going over it again and again in his mind. How he'd line up at the start, when to push, when to lie back and exactly when to hit the throttle and leave the rest in his wake. He'd primed the Challenger for events like this. All the tuning, all the engine work—it wasn't for show. It was for the thrill of pure speed.

Win, and he'd take the purse. Twenty-five grand in cash. After paying Chris his cut, it would be enough to start over, enough to build his own business, enough to reclaim everything he'd lost. But was it worth it? Racing meant risking everything he'd built with Anika and with her family.

Still, he couldn't back down. He'd made his choice. He'd committed. And tonight, he'd see it through. The money could change everything.

She'll understand.

All he had to do was prove one thing: that he was a winner.

Jace glanced over, amused. "You're going to wear a hole in the floorboard at that pace."

Elam snorted but didn't stop tapping his foot. "I'm fine," he muttered. "Just keyed up."

Jace chuckled. "Nervous?"

Elam didn't answer right away. He rubbed his palm over his jeans and stared out the window at the flickering fence posts rushing by.

"Not about the race," he admitted. "Anika."

Jace's smile faded. "Ah."

"We had a fight. A bad one."

"Over tonight?"

Elam nodded, jaw tightening. "She didn't want me to go. Said it was dangerous. Said it was going back to who I used to be."

Jace whistled. "What'd you say?"

"I told her I wanted my *Englisch* life back."

His friend winced. "You said that? Man, what are you doing, trying to win the argument or set the barn on fire?"

"I didn't mean it like that," Elam snapped, then sighed again and slumped in his seat. "She took everything I said wrong, you know?"

Jace snorted. "Yeah, girls usually do."

A hollow ache filled him. Everything good he'd tried to do had gone wrong, and he'd give anything to fix it. "I guess I didn't say things the way I should have," he admitted. "I wanted her to understand why I'm doing this. It's just a onetime thing. I win, I get money and I'm out."

Jace nodded slowly, turning his eyes back to the road. "You told her that?"

"I tried," Elam said. "But I think all she heard was me turning my back on everything we've been building. On her."

"You going to try and fix it?"

Elam nodded. "As soon as I've got that cash in hand. I'll show her this was for us. She'll understand."

"She probably already does," Jace said with a shrug. "She's just scared."

"She has every right to be," Elam said. "I am, too."

Conversation fell into silence after that. The road curved gently through the countryside, lined by tall grass and silhouettes of trees reaching into the night sky. The Dodge purred beneath them, its engine humming with power and promise.

Until it didn't.

Without warning, the hum sputtered, coughed and jolted. The vehicle lurched forward as a grinding wheeze filled the air.

"What the heck—?" Jace's hands gripped the wheel as the car lost power steering. He coasted toward the shoulder, guiding the heavy vehicle with practiced hands. They rolled to a stop on the gravel shoulder, the only sound the ticking of cooling metal.

"I didn't do anything," Jace claimed, lifting his hands sheepishly. "I swear. I was just driving."

Heart hammering, Elam unbuckled his seat belt. "Pop the hood."

Jace did. "Hope it's nothing bad."

"Me, too." Grabbing a flashlight out of the glove compartment, Elam swung open the door, the gravel crunching under his boots as he rounded to the front. He lifted the hood and was immediately hit with the faint warmth of the engine, the oily scent of machinery.

He shined the light. Nothing looked out of place. Battery cables were tight. Spark plug wires were secure. No steam, no leaking fluid, no belt out of place. The oil level was good. Coolant full. Everything was right.

"Try it now," he called.

Jace turned the key. The starter clicked. Whirred. Then stopped.

No turnover.

"Try again."

Click. Whirr. Silence.

Giving up, Jace appeared beside him, peering into the engine bay. "Well?"

"I don't get it," Elam said, shining the light every which way. "It was running fine earlier. I took it down to the gas station and back with no problem."

"Fuel pump?"

"No way. It's new. So's the relay. I tested all of it."

"Maybe vapor lock?"

"Not this time of year. And I've got the tank vented."

Jace shrugged. "You sure nothing's shorting out?"

"I checked everything." Elam gestured helplessly. "It's all fine. It should start and purr like a kitten."

Jace scratched the back of his head. "Yeah, well, it's not."

Leaning into the fender, Elam felt frustration roll over him. So much was riding on tonight. Winning meant Reuben's therapy bills could finally get paid. It meant easing the constant strain Anika carried, trying to stay strong for everyone else.

It meant proving something. To her. To himself.

But the car, a machine he knew from front to back, had quit for no reason.

Anger rising, he glanced toward the wide-open sky. "God, if You're trying to prove something, this isn't funny."

And then, there it was. A gentle pause. A quiet nudge. Not a voice in his ears, but a stirring deep inside, so insistent that it could not be ignored.

This wasn't his path.

The thought struck him so hard he blinked, confused. He looked down at his hands, then at the open hood, then back up at the stars flickering awake overhead.

All this time, he'd been praying for a sign.

And now?

Now, with everything working, everything perfect, the car refused to move another inch.

Like the Lord had reached down and turned the key the other way.

Elam stood beside the car, the ticking of the engine the only sound. A stillness settled over him, deep and undeniable. And in that hush, he felt it. The peace everyone had spoken of. It was just there. Finally.

And then, he knew.

"I'm not supposed to go," he blurted, the words spilling out before he could second-guess them.

Jace looked at him, brows raised. "Come again?"

Elam turned toward him. "God stopped me."

"Okay." Jace frowned. "You mean, like, metaphorically, or…"

"I mean it literally," Elam said. "Tonight, before I left, I prayed and asked the Lord for a sign. I asked if this race was the right thing. And now, when everything should work, it doesn't." Shaking his head, he added, "This doesn't feel random."

Jace laughed, disbelieving. "You think God sabotaged your car?"

"I think the Lord answered my prayer." Elam let out a shaky laugh. "I thought I needed this race. Thought I had to do it to prove myself. But I didn't. I just needed to listen." He'd finally learned the Lord wasn't loud or fierce. He was just there.

Jace stared at him like he'd grown an extra head. "Man, are you sure? You're going to walk away from that much money and a grudge match with Chris Weaver because your car won't start?"

Elam looked down at the Challenger—thirty-six hundred

pounds of raw power, speed and recklessness packed into its sleek frame. And now, it had failed him at the exact moment it mattered most.

But he wasn't angry. He wasn't disappointed.

He was relieved.

"Yeah. I'm sure."

Shaking his head, Jace gave a low whistle. "Well, all right, then. What do we do now?"

Elam pulled his cell phone from his pocket. A single bar, but enough to hopefully get a call into town through. He scrolled through his contacts and tapped the number for his old boss.

"Call a tow," he said. "And wait."

Leaning against the car, Jace snorted. "You know, for a guy who was itching for one last blaze of glory, this is a pretty disappointing ending."

Elam shrugged, watching the signal flicker as the call began to ring. "I reckon so."

The wind picked up, rustling through the trees and lifting the scents of warm earth and roadside grass. Somewhere behind them, a field of fireflies blinked into life. The Challenger sat silent, hood open, still and humbled. No other cars were in sight. The wait promised to be a long one.

Nor was the irony of the moment lost on him. The lesson had come through, and he'd learned it.

When the Lord speaks, a man listens.

But it wasn't the end of his dreams or ambition. It was a new beginning, the start of doing things right.

He intended to do just that. Bend a knee, pray and then listen to what God had to say.

All for the chance to walk a new path.

Anika sat on the edge of her bed, her Bible open but forgotten in her lap. Her gaze was fixed on the window, watching the last flickers of daylight fade behind the distant trees.

Yesterday's argument with Elam pressed heavily on her heart, a dull ache that refused to ease. She'd believed she was protecting them, shielding everyone from reckless dreams and dangerous risks. But now, the memory of Elam's hopeful eyes pierced her heart like a sharp blade. He hadn't wanted the race for the thrill or the glory. It was his desperate fight for a future.

For Daed. For her. For all of them.

And more than anything, he'd said he wanted to marry her.

And I pushed him away.

Her breath caught, tears blurring her vision. Why had she been so blind?

Lowering her head, she closed her eyes and prayed silently, "Lord, how do I fix this? How do I make him see I never meant to break us?"

A soft knock broke the quiet. Nathan's voice followed. "Anika? Can I come in?"

She started, tempted to tell him to go away, but he hadn't done anything wrong. "*Ja*," she called. "You can."

Nathan stepped inside. The warm glow of the lamp on the dresser cast a soft light between them. "You've been here all day," he said, settling onto the chair by the bed.

"Just thinking about Elam," she said, closing her Bible and setting it aside. Since their argument, a heavy weight had settled in her chest. Regret welled up, sharp and raw. "I jumped on him."

Nathan's gaze held steady. "I know you didn't mean to."

"I just didn't agree with the race. It's too dangerous."

"But it meant everything to him," he replied. "One last run to get the money to help *Daed*."

She swallowed hard. "Instead of supporting him, I let him go."

"It's not too late to catch up," Nathan said, leaning forward. "The race won't start until after sundown."

Anika looked up. "How do you know?"

Nathan laughed. "Most everyone does. Word gets around."

It was true. Humble was a small town where Saturday nights stretched long and slow, and though unofficial and against the law, street racing had become a local pastime. Anika had never cared much for it, but she knew Amish folks who listened to sports on the radio or attended local events. Those two brothers who left the community to work on a NASCAR crew were a big deal.

"I guess you're right."

"You don't have to miss it," Nathan added, brightening. "We can still go. I know where it's at—that highway outside the old logging trail. It isn't that far."

She hesitated, worry flickering. "But what if—"

"Nothing's going to happen," he cut in. "*Daed*'s in bed early tonight."

Anika's mouth twitched into a reluctant smile. "Guess you would know that."

Nathan flashed a guilty grin. "We'll stick together, watch the cars, and be back before anyone notices," he said, eyes lighting with excitement.

She nodded, drawing strength from his calm assurance. She wasn't interested in the race. She needed to see Elam, to apologize for the fight. Every second felt heavier. She might lose everything if she let this chance slip.

"Okay," she agreed, pushing off the bed with newfound determination. "Let's go."

Nathan grinned. "I'll hitch the horse." He added, "With his fan going, *Daed* won't hear a thing."

Anika shook her head. If anything, her little brother was a master at sneaking out of the *haus* without getting caught. Like most teens his age, he knew all the tricks.

"You'd better not be wrong," she warned as they closed the back door behind them. The dim outline of the barn loomed in the distance.

Lantern in hand, Nathan returned a confident look. "Trust me. I know where I'm going."

A half hour later, the buggy creaked along the two-lane highway. Mossie's iron-shod hooves struck the asphalt with confidence, pulling them along at a brisk trot. Other vehicles hummed by steadily. Passing them, they were likely headed to the big event of the night.

Anika's heart thudded as she clung to the seat. The buggy's battery-powered headlights cast a wide, strong beam. Nathan guided the mare with steady assurance. She wasn't used to doing things behind her father's back, but a spark of daring flickered to life.

As they rounded a sharp bend, the outlines of a stalled car came into view. Parked by the roadside, the hood was up. Two figures stood beside it, one instantly recognizable.

Anika's breath caught as recognition kicked in. "Is that Elam?"

"Think so," Nathan replied, urging Mossie to slow down before guiding the buggy to a stop behind the car. The mare snorted and pawed at the ground, her ears flicking forward in agitation, as if she sensed the tension in the air.

Worry quickened Anika's steps as she climbed down and hurried toward them. "Elam?"

Bathed in the buggy's headlights, he looked up. "What are you doing here?" His companion waved but stayed silent.

Shivering, Anika glanced at the sleek car. "Nathan wanted to see the race," she explained. "I couldn't let him go alone." She gestured at the exposed engine. "Why is it just sitting here?"

"It broke down," Elam answered, shooting the car a fierce scowl.

Leaning in, Nathan bent to look under the hood. "What happened?"

"Don't know." Shrugging with helpless dismay, Elam swept the flashlight's narrow beam across the dead engine. The light caught on metal and shadow, but nothing gave him a clue. His free hand came down on the edge of the hood, a weary gesture of defeat. "The Dodge just quit for no reason I can see."

Tension easing, Anika exhaled. Relief flickered through her, but so did guilt. He'd wanted this so badly. "I'm sorry. I know how much you wanted to go."

A wry smile tugged. "Looks like the plan changed."

"You can't fix it?" Nathan asked.

"Not in the middle of nowhere," Elam said, letting out a sharp sigh of disgust. "I've looked it over and can't find the problem. Out here in the dark, there's no telling what I'm missing."

Disappointment flashed across Nathan's face. "What now?"

Elam's friend finally spoke up. "We're waiting for a tow to come pick us up." He squinted down the road. "Hope we're not here all night. I have an early shift at work tomorrow."

"Sorry, Jace," Elam said, rubbing the back of his neck. "I'll get you home as soon as I can."

Jace shook his head. "You owe me one, man."

Anika hesitated, glancing between the two before blurting, "I'm glad you didn't make it."

Elam turned to her, surprised. "You are?"

She nodded. "I know how much it means to you. But…the risk… I was worried about you. I don't want to lose you to something bad happening."

His expression changed, the hardness easing. "I didn't think you cared."

"I do," she admitted, knees shaking, pulse thundering. "More than I thought I would."

A faint smile touched his lips, easing the tension between them. "Me, too." He stepped closer, reaching for her hand. His touch was warm, familiar and steadying. "I'm sorry for what I said yesterday. I hope you'll forgive me?"

Hope stirring, Anika's pulse quickened. She squeezed his fingers. "I do."

Elam met her gaze, uncertainty flickering in his eyes. "Can we start over?" he asked. "This time, I promise I'll do things God's way."

Anika's breath caught. The honesty in his words was too vulnerable to be anything but real—and she believed him.

Completely.

"Oh—there's one more thing I need to ask," he added.

"What's that?" she asked, puzzled.

The beam from the flashlight trembled slightly before he steadied it. "You're going to marry me… Right?"

Surprised, she let out a shaky laugh. "Am I?"

"Well, not today." Chuckling, his smile widened. "But someday I intend to make you my *fraa*." He gave her hand a light tug. "If you'll have me."

"Oh, Elam…" she whispered, breathless. "You mean it?"

"I do. And I'll say that, and more, right now under heaven itself." Grinning, he tightened his hold, as if anchoring himself to her. "I love you, Anika Glick."

Tears welled, blurring her vision. "I love you too, Elam Mueller." She'd tried so hard to guard her heart, to keep the walls firm. But they'd never held. Not against him.

Elam gathered her close, his hold steady and sure. "Then it's settled," he murmured, the certainty in his voice wrapping around her like an embrace. He bent, his lips brushing her forehead in a fleeting kiss. Warm and tender, it was a silent vow of brighter days ahead.

Anika willingly leaned into him, letting his words—and his promise—sink in. "*Ja*," she whispered. "It is."

"Ugh. Love," Nathan groaned with mock exasperation in his voice, though his grin gave him away.

Suddenly, the precious moment shattered.

The stillness broke with a scream of sirens, a wailing chorus that cut the air. A police car—and then an ambulance—streaked past in a blur of light, their red and blue reflections flashing over every surface. Farther down the road, a black column of smoke spiraled into the sky, a writhing column of shadowed gray crowned by the flare of orange flames licking at the darkening sky.

"Something bad happened," Jace commented, shivering as he crossed his arms.

Worry furrowed Elam's brow. "Looks like they're heading for the location where the race was supposed to take place."

"Hope no one's hurt," Nathan added, shivering. "I'm glad you didn't make it now."

"Looks like you were right about someone upstairs watching out for you," Jace commented dryly. "I wouldn't have believed it if I hadn't seen it myself."

Watching the emergency vehicles vanish down the road, Anika felt an unexpected calm settle over her.

Everything's going to be all right.

She didn't know how she knew. She just did.

Gott worked in ways no one could predict. Sometimes, what was broken had to fall completely apart before it could be made whole again. Sometimes faith meant walking blindly into the unknown, believing even when the path ahead was veiled in shadows.

Elam's reckless decision had been his way of fighting for their future. But the Lord's plan was always greater than any risk, richer than any reward. His was a path of healing and redemption, of love deeper than fear and forgiveness wide enough to mend even the deepest wounds.

Whispering a quick prayer, Anika leaned into Elam's sturdy frame. In that moment, she didn't see the boy who had made mistakes. She saw the man he was becoming.

Gott wasn't just restoring what had been shattered. He was building something new. Something better.

Not just in Elam.

In her, too.

As they stood side by side in the hush of that uncertain night, her spirit lifted with quiet joy. Love no longer felt like a distant dream.

It felt real. Solid.

And this time, she wasn't afraid to hold on.

Epilogue

One year later...

Sunlight streamed through the tall windows of the community meetinghouse, casting soft light across the smooth wooden floor. Though recently completed, the space felt familiar and grounded. Whitewashed walls, exposed beams and rows of wooden benches gave it a quiet, sturdy character. In keeping with Amish tradition, there were no decorations save for the plain wooden cross above the bishop's lectern.

The space was still, filled with quiet anticipation. The morning sermon and hymns had ended, and the moment everyone had been waiting for had arrived. Bible in hand, the bishop would soon begin the wedding ceremony, spoken entirely in High German, as was tradition. Though no flowers or other decorations adorned the space, there was a purity in its simplicity. A marriage wasn't meant to be elaborate. Rather, it was a covenant rooted in humility, commitment and community.

Elam stood at the front, palms brushing the seams of his best black trousers. His white shirt, neatly pressed, was buttoned to the throat, and the sleeves hugged arms that had known their fair share of labor. The stiff cut of his black coat didn't bother him today. Neither did the stress of so many eyes watching. His gaze was fixed on the rear doors. Breath hitched, nerves taut, he waited. Today, with loved ones all around, he would marry the woman who had captured his heart.

Abram leaned in at his side, teasing, "You sure you're ready?"

Elam snorted. "Wouldn't have gotten dressed up if I weren't."

His older brother grinned, fiddling with his cuffs. "Never thought I'd see this day. The youngest of us all, baptized and getting married."

He grinned. "I didn't, either."

Glancing toward the window, his thoughts carried him back. There was a time he never would've believed this day could come…

After the disastrous night of the race, he'd finally gotten the Dodge towed to the garage and cooled his temper long enough to look it over. The issue had been embarrassingly simple. A disconnected wire, no bigger than a pencil stub. He could have fixed it in a second. But he hadn't seen it the night of the race.

And now, standing here, he smiled to himself.

I wasn't meant to.

Gott had a different plan.

That breakdown had brought him back to the fork in his road. And this time, he'd chosen the right path. He gave up *Englisch* ways. Sold the Challenger, his work truck and the garage. All three had fetched a fair price, too. Enough to pay for Reuben's physical therapy and then some. It was the best decision he'd ever made as an adult, and he was content with his choices.

He was also ready to walk a fresh path, one that would lead him closer to *Gott* and back to his community.

Making good on his promise, he'd rejoined the church. Under Bishop Graber's guidance, he'd completed an intense study of the *Dordrecht Confession of Faith.* A counseling program spanning weeks, the instruction prepared him for his *Dauff.* It hadn't been easy. Facing up to his mistakes and stubborn nature had nearly undone him. But the church elder had a patient way of speaking and a firmer way of waiting.

By the following spring, he'd stood in front of the entire congregation, nervous and shaking but proud, and made his statement of faith. He was baptized. So was Anika.

And that was when the genuine change began.

He'd started his own business, building a custom buggy to suit his new business as a mobile mechanic. The boxy back was fitted with drawers, slots, and racks for tools, parts, and all manner of fix-it odds and ends. Folks called him from all over the county for repairs. He worked hard and was always busy.

As Abram had suggested, he took over his grandfather's old *haus*. It needed work, but he was determined to honor its history while bringing it into the present. He hired the best tradesmen, updating the home with propane appliances, which were safe, efficient and dependable. Solar panels, discreetly tucked into the roofline, provided electricity, a quiet nod to the community's gradual shift toward modern conveniences. Natural sunlight was now welcomed to power homes, farms and businesses. The kerosene lamps were gone, the creaky floorboards replaced. It wasn't fancy, but it was clean, sturdy and waiting to be filled with new memories.

And, someday, the patter of little feet.

Anxious for the ceremony to begin, Elam scanned the faces filling the wooden benches. His siblings were all there. Abram stood as a groomsman, while Rolf, Samuel, Lavinia and Annalise sat with their spouses and little ones in tow. Only one face was missing—his niece Trisha. Last he'd heard, Rolf's oldest daughter had left the community. As the first family member to graduate from the local community college, she'd gone off to chase a career in the *Englisch* world.

Elam's mouth curved. Times were changing, and Amish youths were beginning to branch out into less traditional career paths. Trisha's ambitious pursuit seemed far-fetched, but he couldn't bring himself to judge. Everyone had to make their choices. All he could do was pray that everything would turn out well.

Movement stirred near the rear doors, pulling his attention back to the present. The crowd fell silent, anticipation hanging thick in the air.

One by one, the women chosen as Anika's *newehockers* stepped elegantly down the aisle—Mary Beth Stoltz, Katie Ann Boller and Lizzy Schrock, her closest friends.

Then, framed perfectly in the doorway and bathed in soft light, Anika appeared. Her frock and matching flats were a shade of dusty rose, and her crisp white apron lay smooth and perfectly in place. Her long hair was neatly pinned up beneath a simple white *kapp.* A happy glow flushed her cheeks, and her eyes sparkled. Gripping his walker with steady hands, Reuben stood beside her, upright, strong and proud as ever.

Seeing them together, Elam drew in a breath. Every sacrifice he'd made had led to this moment. Anika was prim and beautiful.

And Reuben? He'd done exactly what he said he would.

Though he needed a mobility aid, he was up. On his own two feet.

"That's our Lord at work," Abram murmured, impressed. "We all prayed Reuben would make it out of that wheelchair."

"It's all thanks to Elam," Nathan said, his voice thick with gratitude. "*Daed* got the therapy he needed."

Embarrassed, he brushed off the praise. "It was my pleasure."

Nathan gave him a poke. "We'll always be indebted."

Elam returned the playful gesture, nudging back. "That's what we're meant to do. We take care of each other." Every word carried his wholehearted conviction.

"Indeed, we do," Abram said, beaming proudly.

Though it wasn't the usual tradition, Anika had asked Bishop Graber to let her father accompany her down the aisle. Together, they proceeded slowly, but steadily. Reuben leaned hard on his walker, each step etched with pain and grit. He wasn't fully healed. But seeing him make it this far stirred hope in the entire congregation.

Elam's throat tightened as the pair drew closer. Reuben's steps were uneven, but he never wavered. Anika stayed close, her hand resting lightly on his arm, her face radiant with joy.

He didn't deserve any of it. Not this girl. Not her family. Not the second chance he'd been given. But that was the beauty of *Gott*'s mercy. It came not where it was earned, but where it was needed most.

Thank You, Lord, for making this day possible.

As their walk came to an end, Reuben steadied himself. "Today, I am not giving away my *dochder*," he said in *Deitsch*, his voice strong despite the quiver in his frame. "I am gaining a *sohn*. Welcome to the *familie*."

Elam responded, "*Ich fühle mich geehrt.* And I promise to take *gut* care of her."

Reuben smiled, then carefully made his way to the front row.

Elam extended a hand to his bride. "You ready?"

"*Ja.*" Anika's fingers tightened around his. "I am."

Together, they faced Bishop Graber.

A gentle smile touched the older man's lips. "It fills my heart to see the faith and strength you have both grown into." With that, he began the ceremony.

The service that followed was simple, honoring the traditions passed down through the ages. Their vows were clear and solemn. Promises spoken not just to each other, but before *Gott* and their people.

When the last echo of their promises settled, Bishop Graber's smile deepened. "You may seal your union with a kiss," he said, his voice carrying both a blessing and quiet joy.

Elam turned to Anika, their eyes meeting in silent understanding. No words were needed. He smiled, and she countered with one of her own. Then, in perfect sync, they leaned in and kissed.

The crowd responded with soft clapping and murmured blessings. A few of the younger spectators even cheered. Bishop Graber allowed the celebration, for the day was a joyous one for all.

As they stood there, Elam felt a deep sense of peace settle in his soul. He wasn't the man he used to be, lost and drifting. He was a man of faith now. A man who had found his place, his purpose, and his people.

Beside him stood the woman who had helped him to believe again. And ahead of them stretched a blessed future he could finally embrace with open hands and a willing heart.

Forever.

* * * * *

Dear Reader,

I'm thrilled to welcome you back to Humble, Wisconsin, where the simplicity of Amish life sets the stage for these heartfelt stories. In *Her Reluctant Amish Heart*, the third book in the Humble Blessings series, I invite you to join Elam Mueller and Anika Glick on their journey of redemption and hope.

Elam, a young man who turned away from his Amish roots, now stands at a crossroads, grappling with the consequences of his past decisions. Anika, wounded and vulnerable, carries the weight of her family's struggles. When their paths cross, their story becomes one of healing, forgiveness and the quiet miracles that unfold as they learn to trust God's plan.

If you've read earlier books in the series, you'll notice a few familiar faces returning as Elam and Anika step into the spotlight. Writing their story was especially meaningful, as I believe their story of second chances is a reminder that even in our darkest moments, faith can light the way forward. My prayer is that this book leaves you inspired by the power of love, the strength of community and the courage to embrace new beginnings.

If you'd like to keep up with future releases, you can sign up for my newsletter at www.pameladesmondwright.com. You can also drop me a note at PO Box 165, Texico, NM 88135-0165.

Thank you for inviting my stories into your home and heart!

With gratitude,
Pamela Desmond Wright